Earth Legacy
BIRTHRIGHT

LAURIE RYAN

www.laurieryanauthor.com

EARTH LEGACY SERIES

Survival
Enlightenment
Birthright

Earth Legacy
BIRTHRIGHT

LAURIE RYAN

DEDICATION

To Dawn, who always
helps me see
the bright side of life.

PROLOGUE

Taegar thrust her hands into the stream of light that emanated from the floor. Power infused her. Strong, heady power. This was what she wanted. This was her destiny. Boundless power. She swelled with it, let it lift her from the ground as she consumed it like sacred sustenance. She floated there, almost incorporeal, awash in Earth's *awen*, the magic she coveted beyond anything else.

Regretfully, Taegar removed her hand. While stronger than the magic in her cave, the magic here seemed stifled as well. Until she possessed the complete rune set, she must remain patient. That talisman, designed to keep her from magic rightfully hers, must be found. Her golden eyes brightened as she glared at the stones. So many, yet so few. Several were missing, held by her enemy, Rianthe Royan. Daughter to those who'd scorned her all those years ago.

The overland trip to this cave, her first travel of any kind in many, many years, had depleted most of her power. So little remained of her body—the one she'd been born with more than one hundred and twenty years ago—that she could only move with the aid of magic. But the risk had worked in her favor, for she was born anew in this place that Damian and Valena Royan thought to hide from her. There could be no hiding. As soon as she ripped the remaining runes from that girl's lifeless body and released the limitless magic Earth had hidden away, she would bind it to herself for all time. She would be unbeatable. She was nearly that now.

And it felt very, very good.

"I am Taegar," she said to the empty cave. "I am the *isa*, that which provides clarity to the world and bends it to my righteous path. I am *thurisaz*, creator of chaos, and *tiwaz*, ruler of all. I *am* the Dark circle."

Things were coming to a head. Soon, she would confront the one who stood between her and her destiny. Soon, she would have what she needed to complete her metamorphosis from Dark druid to immortal god. She would have everything she'd waited for all these years.

Very, very soon.

PROVOCATION

CHAPTER ONE

Rianthe shot out of bed, knife in hand, gasping. Any peaceful sleep she'd hoped for had been shattered, but by what? She reached out. The wall behind her was familiar. She was in her bedroom. The surrounding shadows held their normal nuances of gray and black. No imminent danger lurked. Rianthe sank into her bed, laid the knife down, and tried to determine what terror had set her off.

Taschia whined, the wolf who'd been her steadfast companion for the past three years always concerned about her welfare.

Rianthe laid a hand on her head. "I'm all right, sister-wolf. It was only a nightmare."

The wolf cocked her head as she mind-spoke. *Your heart races.*

To honor her sister-wolf, Rianthe communicated the same way, explaining that she would calm in a moment. Taschia took her friend at her word and curled back up on the floor of their sleeping quarters.

Unfortunately, Rianthe did not relax so easily. There had been a time when dark dreams of her parents' deaths had attacked her each and every night. Why had these memories returned to her now?

Rianthe scrubbed at her face, trying to clear the cobwebs from her muddled thoughts long enough to remember what she'd seen in this night's dreams.

Golden eyes. That's what she'd seen. The bright, malevolent eyes that stole her breath, rendered her speechless and all but powerless. The eyes of Taegar, who had caused her parent's deaths and razed their home and most of New Hope to the ground. So many had died because of the Dark druid's quest to bind Earth and its powerful *awen* to herself. Taegar, whom Rianthe had promised to seek out and destroy. Except this had been a Taegar she'd never seen before. Even in her cloaked and formless shell, she stood luminous, awash in a magical light. Beautiful. Deadly.

The increased brightness surrounding Taegar meant her strength had somehow grown tenfold. This spelled disaster for Rianthe. For New Hope. For the whole of humanity.
Wide awake now, Rianthe vividly recalled the scene that had torn her from a deep sleep. Taegar, staring right at her, her eyes ablaze. "Come to me. Bring me the talisman." Honey dripped from the voice that beckoned Rianthe.

Yet it hadn't been the voice that caused Rianthe's reaction. In this dream, the light called to her. Radiant light, dazzling power. She gazed at the beauty of Earth's pure essence, tears streaming down her face.

Rianthe rose from the ground and raised her hand

toward the light, unable to stop herself. She must touch this pureness of this energy and bond with it. A symbiosis of love and joy and power.

"Come to me," the disembodied voice repeated. "I am the only one you need."

"No," Rianthe whispered, not taking her eyes from the stream of light. "You are not what I need." One step. Two. Rianthe moved forward, toward the energy that shone so brightly. She needed to be part of this beauty. Reaching out, she touched it and was filled with heady power, a good magic that filled her with wonder. Filled her with love...

The power grew within her, but not fast enough. Earth's *awen* poured into her, an all-encompassing strength grown from everything good in Earth's core. If Rianthe missed the almost imperceptible murkiness at the edges of the light, she could be forgiven. Nothing mattered but becoming one with Earth and evolving into what she'd been born to become.

The splendor distracted her, giving the darkness time to grow. Soon, it swallowed the goodness and love until there was only an elixir of dark power that pulled at Rianthe. She needed more, needed to feed the darkness consuming her soul. All of her good intentions faded away. She desired more, and that lust filled her until there was no more space. Still, Rianthe demanded more. Darkness spread through the light, expanding as she bent the magic to her will.

A mirror leaned against a rock wall. Rianthe turned and saw...herself, yet not herself. Awash in light, an aura of power surrounded her, flowing in waves from brilliant golden eyes.

Eyes very like those of her enemy. Taegar's eyes.

Her eyes.

Rianthe shook herself from her memory and realized she was trembling like a wolf pup on a cold night. She wished she could turn to Kaiden Darcy for solace. He was her closest friend and ally, the man who'd protected her all these years. But he wasn't there. It seemed so long ago that Kaiden had helped her through her nightmares. When he'd comforted and supported her. She missed that. She missed him, more than she should admit.

Rianthe took deep, slow breaths, trying to calm her still-racing heart. She'd had so many nightmares in her life, yet this new, more powerful dream shocked her. Was it a portent? An omen? In the dream, she'd given in to Taegar, which made little sense. Rianthe had seen her fate in the *ehwaz*, the vision plane. Her destiny was to die freeing the *awen* from whatever bound it. This nightmare, though, hadn't felt like death. More a dark rebirth.

Which future was correct?

Walking to the door of the rebuilt druid's tower where she'd been ensconced by the people of New Hope, Rianthe looked out at the night. She contemplated the prophecy that had set her fate in motion.

Shattered by darkness the magic vanished.
It lays in wait for one who's banished.
Hidden power will blossom anew.
Only by passing the darkness through.

Bhren, the Guardian druid who'd taken her in as an apprentice, believed the prophecy spoke of her. But doubts about her abilities had plagued him. She'd seen worry in his face right up until he'd lost the Forever breath, and Bhren had died before he explained just how she was supposed to free Earth's hidden powers and heal their world.

Rianthe clutched her shirt to her chest for warmth against the late winter cold. Spring was only weeks away, yet they seemed mired in an endless winter. She stoked the fire to warm the room, then stared into the flames. So much doubt remained, mostly hers, over whether she truly was this prophesied one. Most of New Hope believed what Bhren had told them. He'd brought those with any magical ability together here to await the fulfillment of the prophecy.

The last of the original Guardian circle had decided on his deathbed to pass on the mantle of Guardian druid to her. He'd given her the signet ring of his circle to prove to all that she was their final hope. Yet she didn't completely trust his conviction. She had power, but not nearly enough, and she'd wasted so much time thinking only about herself. When Bhren and Kaiden had betrayed her, she'd run away instead of asking their reasons. She'd run hard and fast, straight to the Fringes, a lawless area that disavowed magic of any kind. It had taken dire consequences to drive her back to New Hope and the destiny she could no longer deny.

So many years wasted. Years she should have spent developing abilities and learning how to defeat the Dark druid and thus return hope to humankind. Rianthe had squandered much in her short twenty-three years. Too much wasted time.

A log settled in the fireplace, sending up a shower of sparks. Rianthe pushed the logs back with a stick. This gloomy reminiscence got her nowhere since the past could not be changed. Hope lay with the future. She must devote more time and energy to gaining strength, to building a solid belief in herself and her abilities, and to learning how to funnel what magic she had into a formidable weapon against the darkness.

Settling back down on her cot, Rianthe closed her eyes, trying to find some peace in sleep. Constantly under fire from visions and dreams, as well as reality, there seemed no escape. And this dream? Well, it reinforced that Rianthe did not yet have the strength or power needed for the coming battle. She would succumb. If not to Taegar's overwhelming power, then to her own shallow needs. The power had been tangible. She'd touched it, consumed it. She'd wanted it to consume her.

Taegar seemed stronger in this dream than in any previous vision in which she and Rianthe had fought. How? That shouldn't have happened. Unless the talisman had helped her? Rianthe clutched the bag of runes around her neck. Only three remained. The rest of the set now lay in Taegar's dangerous hands. It galled Rianthe that she'd lost them. Her first true test of strength and she'd failed. Taegar's acolyte had taken them from her as easily as separating leaves from a dying tree. Worse, that battle had almost killed Kaiden.

Was this nightmare a portent of things to come or a sign of what had already come to pass? Rianthe tried hard to dredge up more of the fading dream. The light in the cave had seemed stronger than in prior visions. Taegar's cave had manifested a stream of white magic, but it had been weak. This was much stronger. Rianthe fought through the fading scenes in her mind and looked around the cave she'd assumed was the same one where she'd met Taegar before.

What if this wasn't Taegar's cave?

All the breath whooshed from Rianthe's lungs. Her

pulse pounded, her heart pushing blood through her so fast that her skin tingled. Had Taegar found Origin cave? Was the book harbored there, the one left there for her by her parents, safe?

Rianthe threw on some clothes, ran down the stairs and straight to the little building beside the tower, now sleeping quarters for one.

"Kaiden."

His eyes opened. Kaiden the protector rarely slept. At least, not well. The man was always alert.

"What's up? What's wrong?" he said, reaching for his knife.

"We need to talk. Jonah and Roulf should be in on this, too."

Her resolve must have cleared any confusion in Kaiden's mind. He stood without another question. "I'll get Jonah. You get Roulf. Meet us in the dining house."

While Kaiden went for Jonah, his father and the village elder, Rianthe flew to the tent Roulf had constructed near the growing fields. The little man who'd become her mentor didn't like people much, though he'd grown used to living around the inhabitants of New Hope since he'd left his solitary abode to help them. At the end of the day, he preferred the solitude of the woods. Rianthe appreciated that. In fact, she felt the same way quite often.

"Roulf," she called.

The tent flap opened and Roulf stepped out, clothed and ready to go.

"You're dressed," she said.

"I knew you were coming."

"How did you— Never mind. That's not important. We need to talk."

"Yes. Kaiden and Jonah are waiting for us."

Roulf hurried off to meet the other men. Rianthe followed more slowly. From the first time she'd met the man, when she'd fallen into his cabin in the midst of a snowstorm, he'd been an enigma. Short by any standard, he could bend air, morphing it into whatever he wanted something to look like, even turning himself into a bear of a man for defense purposes. And that wasn't all. The man who'd once been a student of the Guardian druids always seemed aware of what was going on, sometimes before it happened. It was a mystery she'd never been able to figure out.

She didn't understand him, but she remained grateful he was there. And tonight wasn't the night to figure Roulf out. Rianthe quickened her pace. They had dangerous things to discuss.

CHAPTER TWO

Inside the long, thatch-roofed building that served as kitchen, dining, and meeting space, Kathra poured wake-up draughts into cups. Rianthe smelled the strong brew with appreciation. The red-headed mother of Rianthe's equally red-headed friend Mokie had an innate ability to turn sludge into palatable food that was nothing short of magical. The scent calmed Rianthe's nerves even as her insides rumbled with a churning worry over the knowledge she'd gleaned from her nightmare.

"How come you're up this early?" she asked Kathra, grateful for even a moment's distraction from the new danger she'd soon have to speak of.

Kathra leaned in. "I saw Jonah and Raisa head this way. Figured this time of the morning, it wasn't good and they'd need some fortitude."

"You are very right," Jonah said, sitting down across from Rianthe. He picked up his cup to sip the hot brew.

Everyone else sank to the benches on either side of the table. Kaiden patted the shoulders of both Jonah and Raisa, the foster parents who'd raised him, as he came around to sit next to Rianthe. Roulf sat on the other side of Rianthe, and Raisa motioned for Kathra to sit next to her. No one else was around at this unearthly hour except the ever-present Taschia, who slipped under the table to lie on the floor, warming Rianthe's feet against the late-winter chill.

"What happened?" Jonah asked without preamble.

"I had a nightmare," Rianthe said.

Kaiden looked at her with alarm. "I thought you'd stopped having those."

"I did. Or, at least, I had up until tonight. That's not important. What's important is that..." Rianthe's voice trailed off. She hated to even put words to her thoughts, but she had to. "I think Taegar has found Origin cave."

The collective silence around the table validated the severity of the situation. Rianthe, Roulf, and Taschia had found Origin cave a few weeks before. Rianthe's parents had tried to take their family to the cave years earlier, as they fled from Taegar They'd been unsuccessful. They died in front of Rianthe when she'd been only ten years old.

"This was a dream. How certain can you be?" Jonah asked.

"Very." She knew that cave inside and out from all the days she'd spent training there with Roulf, training she'd aborted to rescue Kaiden and find her brother. Rianthe wrung her hands under the table, hoping she wouldn't have to explain the rest. She didn't understand herself how she had been lured into that darkness. Except she hadn't been lured. She'd reached for it, wanting it more than anything or anyone she'd ever wanted in her life, including Kaiden.

No. She wasn't ready to talk about that part of her dream. Not until she had proof that she would not succumb. Until her powers matured to the point where she would not surrender to that yearning.

"I agree with her," Kaiden said. "I've seen her reactions to these nightmares. They're more like her visions than a sleep-induced memory."

Rianthe glanced at him gratefully while Roulf sat rubbing his chin, pondering.

"We have to do something," Rianthe said. "I've told you about the magic stream in that cave. It's like the one in Taegar's, only stronger."

Roulf nodded his agreement.

"If she's reached that—" Rianthe didn't finish the sentence. She didn't need to. They knew. Taegar, in her current state, was a nearly unstoppable force. With added power? Rianthe stifled a shudder, glancing out the doorway to the new day just beginning to dawn. "We have to stop her."

"How?" Jonah asked, frustration filling his voice. "I can't even imagine how we can accomplish that, but I'm open to suggestions."

Every set of eyes focused on her, but she had no idea. Once again, the weight of action lay on her shoulders. She was the Guardian druid. The one with the power. Yet she'd almost been destroyed by the woman sent by Taegar to convert Kaiden to the Dark circle. She wasn't ready. She needed more time, more training.

No one else had any more power than she did, though. That was the second problem.

Kaiden squeezed her shoulder and turned her to face

him. He knew her better than anyone. Kaiden had been her best friend and confidant ever since she'd fallen into New Hope all those years ago. Sure, they'd had a falling out. Well, actually, she'd run away for five years to the last place magic would find her. Since then, their relationship had been tremulous. Maybe they could rebuild what they had. Maybe not. Either way, she appreciated his recognition of the tough spot she was in.

They were all in.

Jonah took another sip of his warm drink and tapped Rianthe's hand. "Let's go over what happened in Minor Town again. You said Marta had power that surprised you, yet you defeated her."

"It took both Kaiden and me to do it," Rianthe said.

"Tell me again how that happened."

"Marta fired magic after magic at me. I stopped hers and created my own fireballs to return her volleys. That's more than I've ever done before. But she never even slowed down. I was weakening, and then—" Rianthe gulped, twirling a strand of hair around her finger over and over again. When she realized what she was doing, she moved her hands to her lap and clenched them under the table.

Taschia nudged her leg. *It is done. I live because of you and Kai-den. Do not worry.*

Kaiden smiled and patted the wolf's head under the table, indicating he'd heard too. Mind-speak with the wolves was not an ordinary power. Most did not have that ability. Plus, the animals selectively closed off those with the ability to hear, speaking to one or many. Or none at all.

"Kaiden got to my side and reached for my hand." Rianthe rubbed her always-gloved hands in her lap. "I didn't have my gloves on."

He reached for her hand now, squeezing through her glove, while everyone nodded. It was common knowledge that direct contact with Earth brought Rianthe to the *ehwaz*, the in-between where life-altering visions occurred. She shuddered as a chill permeated her. The visions always meant pain for her, and tended to have dire consequences. She'd learned that on more occasions than she wanted to think about.

"What changed when he did that?" Roulf asked.

"When we touched, it was...as if we were one person. His energy, his powers to protect flowed into me, adding to my magic, to Earth's *awen*, strengthening it."

She glanced at Kaiden.

The look on his face said it all. There might never be an explanation for what had happened, but they'd grown closer because of it.

"All of a sudden," she continued, "I was stronger than Marta. I loosened her grip on Taschia. I won the battle." Rianthe saw no need to mention she'd thrown Marta against a wall with thought alone. That had been pure revenge for almost killing her sister-wolf. "Marta escaped while we worried over Taschia. I'd expected her to be down for a while. She was pretty beaten up."

"Hmm." Jonah stroked his winter beard. "If she and Taegar are both in Origin cave, it amplifies our problem."

"I could try to divine what's happening through a vision." Rianthe swallowed against the tremor in her voice. "But if Taegar is indeed stronger and connects to my vision, we may give away more than learn."

"Agreed," Roulf said with a sigh. "I think it is time for us to test our strength."

Rianthe put her head in her hands. It seemed their

only option was to search out Taegar and confirm what she'd seen in her dream.

Roulf reached across the table and clutched both her arms. "I'm sorry, child. I know the onus is on your shoulders and the danger is grave. You have the power. It will come to you when you need it."

"It had better, because right now, I can barely lift a rock when I focus. You saw, Roulf. When we were at Origin cave. I can't do it. Not without Kaiden."

He nodded. "Agreed. The magic does not come to you when you are stressed and unable to concentrate. Free of those issues, you can embed said rock in a tree."

Everyone looked at Rianthe, including Kaiden. There was nothing else to do but admit it, so she nodded. "I got angry," she said with a shrug.

"And we've been practicing over the winter. You've shown improvement."

"Yes, now I can raise a rock and a feather in the air at the same time," she said, her words sharpened by bitterness.

"I have long considered your focus to be blocked by other concerns," Roulf continued. "You do better when thrown into a situation than when you prepare for it." He shook his head. "I don't understand why that is. And, while it's not the wisest plan, we have to rely on your ability to rise to the occasion as has been shown each time you've needed it and are unprepared."

"Which means we're back to me being the world's savior, and I've little control over the magic to back that up."

Roulf lifted a forefinger.

"With a bit more control," Rianthe corrected, rising from the table. "I need a minute."

They all watched her closely. She sighed.

"I won't run off and cry in my stew like last time. It's just...I need to think."

They let her go. Rianthe tried not to run as she left the longhouse. She rounded the corner to the back where she'd be alone. Crouching down, she grabbed her stomach and gave into the panic working very hard to consume her. How would she ever do this? How could they ask her to? She was only twenty-three years old, still trying to find herself. Dram. She pounded her legs. What was she going to do?

No. This was too much to ask. She'd taken on Taegar's acolytes and barely escaped with her life. Their lives. Even with Kaiden's help, they'd almost perished. They both had the scars to prove it. Yet Jonah, Roulf, and everyone else expected her to take on the one who held more power than any of them?

She couldn't do it.

Rianthe stood, peeked around the corner, and saw the village awakening. Maybe, if they started a search of their own like Bhren had done all those years ago, they might find someone stronger than her.

Except...they were out of time. And Bhren had already put the stupid idea in everyone's head that she was the one who would save them.

A wolf ran past. Hark, one of her little brother Tevy's pack. Two more followed. Marin and Joek, most likely. As expected, the tan and gray wolf that was her brother came next, a newly forged shape-shifter. He stopped and cocked his head to look at her.

You can do this, Sis. I believe in you.

In a flash, he was off following his brothers. Then, Grog came sauntering along, a piece of meat hanging out of his mouth, his mother Sarsa nudging him from behind. Rianthe almost laughed. Good old Grog, the runt of the litter. The wolf always seemed to be trying to pack on weight to catch up to his brothers. Except he'd overtaken them long ago.

I believe in you. Tevy's mind-spoken words sobered Rianthe. That was the crux of the matter. Everyone believed Bhren had been right. She was the lone holdout.

So be it. Rianthe would accept the challenge and try her best. It was the only way anyone had a chance. She would take on Taegar. There really was no other option.

Resolved, Rianthe walked back inside to the hopeful faces, knowing that no hope would surmount the fact that their chances were less than slim. They were all but non-existent. Maybe this was it, when what she'd seen in one of her visions would come to pass. Maybe this was when she would die in order to save the world.

CHAPTER THREE

Kaiden threw his pack together. He'd done it so often it was routine nowadays. While he hated to leave home, necessity was a burden he must bear.

When Rianthe told them she intended to go, the expression on her face had worried him. He knew that look. Despair. He'd mirrored that sentiment too many times. This was a doomsday quest. Bhren had declared Kaiden True-Named protector on his eighteenth birthday. Now, six years later, he'd failed at just about every attempt to protect those he loved. Except this last time, in Minor Town, when not only Rianthe had been at risk but also many vulnerable children. The younglings, sold or bartered into slavery, had worked the mines under horrible conditions. He'd saved them. That was the first time he'd truly protected anyone.

Now, he would accompany Rianthe to fight in the den of the lion. Rianthe's power was hit and miss. There was no knowing if she'd be capable. And it was his job to protect her.

Kaiden hefted his pack and walked outside, taking a moment to look around New Hope. To an outsider, the place must look like a collection of burned-out shells not yet rebuilt, but he saw the twice-fortified dining house, the druid's tower where each rock in the two stories had been laid by hand. The gardens off in the distance were just starting to sprout the foods that would keep them all alive. And, beyond that, the Remembrance fields, honoring the many who had lost their lives defending New Hope.

This resilient village had taken him in as an orphaned infant and had raised him as one of its own. He'd protect it to the best of his ability. With his life, if need be.

He hoped he'd make it back there, to once again pick up the mantle of protection for this home he loved.

Bucking up his shoulders, he joined the small group in the round, the village center. Jonah stood talking to Roulf, who would go with Rianthe and himself. Taschia would, too. The wolf rarely left Rianthe's side for long anyhow. Besides, Taschia had proven herself a good fighter. Rianthe and the wolf had spent a few years working out their system in the Fringes, a land of outcasts. They fought well together. They'd need help from everyone on this one.

Kaiden's stomach churned. This quest had disaster written all over it.

"You ready?" Rianthe joined him.

He wanted to say yes, but instead, shook his head. "I don't think we'll ever be ready for this." He touched her cheek. "You ready?" he asked.

"As ready as I can be." She glanced away. "If you

listen to Roulf, he doesn't think preparation and practice work for me."

Kaiden tugged a strand of her hair. "That explains all the times you tried to dodge sword practice." He loved sparring with her. She was the only one who even came close to testing his abilities.

"Only because I never beat you."

"You've come close."

His comment put a smile on her face. If he let it, her smile could make him giddy, but other things needed their attention. Still, Kaiden hoped one day they might think about each other instead of the fate of New Hope and the world.

Roulf and Jonah joined them.

"We'll be with you in spirit," Jonah said, pulling each into a hug. "I wish I could go along."

"Your *awen* is better utilized here, father. Our homes still need repair."

New Hope, hit first by a man-made fire they hadn't been able to extinguish, and then by an earthquake for which there'd been no defense, had turned into a very resilient place. Still, they all wondered when this constant barrage would end.

Jonah nodded, reluctant to let either of them go. "Be careful. Be safe. And come home." He clapped them both on the shoulder, then stepped back.

"No sense in delaying," Roulf said. "Based on your vision, Rianthe, Taegar grows stronger. The longer we wait, the more opportunity she has to grow her powers further."

Kaiden nodded. The day had barely begun and no one yet stirred. Only Jonah, Raisa, Tevy, and the wolves were there to see them off.

"We're coming with you," Tevy said.

Everyone turned to gape at him.

"Oh, no, you're not," Rianthe said. "That's a ridiculous idea."

"It's not ridiculous. You'll need us."

"You're twelve years old!"

"Not in wolf form. I'm full-aged and strong. Stronger than anything." Tevy puffed out his chest to prove it.

"I don't care. You're not going."

Uh oh. When Rianthe used that tone of voice, things were about to get serious. Kaiden's ears still burned from her lashings.

"You can't stop me," Tevy said, defiance underlining every word.

Rianthe grabbed him by the shoulders. "Yes, I can." She glanced at Hark.

"Even if you get the wolves to keep me here, I'll follow as soon as I can. You can't make me stay. I can help and I'm going to. We all can." He motioned to the pack of wolves standing behind him.

As much as Kaiden disliked having one more person to protect on this journey, this discussion was rather enjoyable. He stepped back and crossed his arms to watch because Rianthe was perilously close to losing an argument. This might be a first.

"Tevy, I can't focus on the task we need to complete and worry about you at the same time," Rianthe said.

That was probably her most effective argument. It had merit, but the same Royan stubbornness shone in Tevy's eyes. He wasn't buying it.

"You don't have to protect me. I can take care of myself."

"No."

"Yes."

They stood there, nose-to-nose, at a complete impasse.

Kaiden heard what amounted to a throat-clearing in his head.

He is strong, Taschia mind-spoke. *My brothers have been testing him.*

Absolutely not.

Taschia rubbed up against Tevy, then Rianthe. *You cannot stop him from following you.*

"Gah!" Rianthe threw up her hands. She'd lost the argument. Kaiden knew how she felt and privately, he agreed with her. Still, he smiled. This was rare territory for her, losing arguments. She pulled Tevy to her, making him stare her in the eyes. "If you're stronger in wolf form, you stay wolf while we're anywhere near Origin cave. And you stay with your pack."

Tevy bobbed his head up and down. Taking a twelve-year-old on this journey didn't set right with any of them. Tevy, however, was no ordinary child. He never had been and never would be.

Rianthe turned to Hark. "I'm alpha for the duration of this quest. You follow my orders."

Hark growled but canted his head in slow acquiescence.

"You keep him safe," she said. "I'm counting on you. On all of you."

Hark tapped her leg with a paw.

Taschia interpreted. *Our brother will be with us. We will keep him safe.*

"You'd better." She glared at Hark.

With that decided, it was time for goodbyes. New

Hope was stirring. Better to get on their way than be delayed by more leave-taking. Kaiden hugged his mother.

"Come back safe," Raisa said, tears filling her eyes.

He smiled. "I am True-Named protector."

"Make sure you protect yourself, too, then."

Raisa moved to hug Rianthe and Roulf as Jonah stepped beside Kaiden. He clapped his son's shoulder again and pulled him in for one last brief hug. No words were needed between them. This was a dangerous endeavor and all anyone could do now was pray that they all made it home safe and sound.

Kaiden prayed more than anyone.

CHAPTER FOUR

Silence reigned during their journey to the cave. Silence and worry. Rianthe, at Roulf's insistence, floated a rock in the air ahead of her.

"Practice can never hurt," the little man said "To be at your strongest, you must be connected to Earth, so your magic is available at all times."

Her control over the rock pleased her. It floated, bobbing along in front of her like a gull floating on air drafts high in the sky. Pleasure was foreign to her these days. Just about everything added to her worry. Rianthe couldn't shake the idea that something awful was about to happen. She hated that Tevy had come with them. If anything happened to him, she'd never forgive herself.

The rock dropped like the stone it was, barely missing Hark as it hit the ground with a thud. Everyone jerked toward the noise, and a warm flush spread over her cheeks at her lapse in concentration. Roulf crossed his arms over his chest and shook his head, gesturing for her to resume.

The rock rose smoothly into the air and moved forward again, and Rianthe tried very hard not to assume that the quiet talk around her had anything to do with her ability to save them, or lack thereof.

Hark bared his teeth, passing under and beyond the rock with a quick leap. Tevy's wolf-tongue lolled out the side of his mouth as he passed her.

You're laughing at me, she mind-spoke.

Only a little, Tevy answered, then loped away. *It was funny.*

Even Tevy's mental laughter couldn't keep Rianthe's thoughts from drifting to that horrible day when their home had burned down. They'd lost their dear brother Uja when Taegar's man, Deakon, had brought reinforcements and set fire to New Hope.

Rianthe refused to lose Tevy. She couldn't, and that worry added to her sense of doom. She didn't know how to shake it off. She was ready for the coming showdown, so worrying did nothing to help. The rock wobbled, but Rianthe quickly righted it. For now, her attention needed to be there.

In camp each night, they considered the strategies that might give them an edge. She and Roulf knew the layout of Origin cave inside and out. Not that Kaiden cared. He rejected her decision to lead the way at the cave, forgetting—again—that she could protect herself. No one else need be in harm's way, not even him. And yet, they were all walking into the maw of the enemy and would not have a sure plan until they arrived.

She and Roulf mapped the area and planned how they should arrange themselves. Rianthe and Kaiden would slip in and surveil the cave. Ideally, they'd then regroup and formulate a plan. Things were never ideal where Taegar was concerned, but it was a start.

As the day's light faded, they approached the clearing that had set Rianthe on this path. Her third time there. At ten years old, she'd watched her parents die in that clearing, and had run away with her brothers to escape Taegar, the Dark druid. She and Roulf had found this place again on their way to what they now knew to be Origin cave. The pain of both those days touched her heart with sadness.

Rianthe approached the oak tree, pulling off her glove as she neared. Without hesitation, she placed her hand on the tree, hoping against hope that she might talk to her father one more time.

"Father," she whispered.

The tree shivered, but she had no clue whether the breeze or her voice initiated it. Where once she'd been able to communicate with her father through this tree, now only silence met her.

Pulling off her other glove, she leaned against the tree and encircled its young girth with both her hands. This time, her grief wasn't overwhelming. Instead, a gentle sadness filled her at the loss of a much-beloved father.

She glanced at the second oak tree a few yards away. She'd lost both parents that day.

"Ri, you all right?"

Tevy, back in human form, asked the question quietly, as if afraid to lessen the specialness of this place. Rianthe may have lost her parents there, but she'd also gained a brother. Tevy. The only brother she had left now.

Rianthe let go of the tree with one final pat and pulled Tevy into her arms. "I'm all right. It's just...sad, being here again."

"This is the place, isn't it? Where our mother and father died?"

Nodding, Rianthe sat at the base of the tree. "And where you were born." She smiled.

Tevy sat beside her. For a while, they watched as Kaiden and Roulf set up camp.

"I wish I'd known them," he said.

Rianthe hadn't told Tevy anything about his parents until recently, to keep their heritage hidden. When he'd returned to New Hope a changeling, the time had seemed right. "I already told you both our parents were Guardian druids," she said. "That's why we can tap into the *awen*. From what little I know, they were strong in their powers. Especially Father. He was blond, like you."

Rianthe ruffled Tevy's hair and he ducked.

"Aw, come on, Sis. I'm too old for that."

"You will never be too old," she answered, chuckling. "There's a lot of both our parents in you, Tevy. You've always seemed wiser than your years. Father was like that. Quiet, biding his time, but ready with sage advice when needed. Mother, she was a healer and empath. She knew when someone, or something, wasn't right. Again," Rianthe said, briefly touching Tevy's hand, "a lot like you."

Tevy smiled. "I wish I'd known them."

"I wish you had, too," she said, hugging her brother. "These trees and my memories are all we have left of them."

Tevy cocked his head to look up at the wintering oak. "I'd say we have more than that. We have their values, their sense of right and wrong. And their gift of magic. We have the *awen*."

Rianthe nodded, looking north, toward Origin cave. "I just hope it's enough."

"It will be. You've had 'enough' before. You saved Kaiden and that town."

"I dredged something up, but not without help. And yes, I'm getting stronger. Still, I wish I had what you have. An instant power. I envy you that."

His chuckle was muted. "You wouldn't if you'd gone through what I did that first time."

He'd told her bits and pieces about those dark days when he'd gone off on his own to shift-change for the first time. Days when she'd been trying to learn magic and Kaiden had been searching for Tevy. "I never wanted you to know pain like that."

"It was worth it." A young boy's enthusiasm shone through in Tevy's voice.

"It doesn't still hurt, does it? When you change into your wolf?"

"Not a bit. And I'm getting faster, too. See?" Tevy leaped into the air and before his paws hit the dirt, he was wolf. He turned a sloppy grin to Rianthe.

She laughed and slapped his hindquarters. "All right, go run off some steam with that pack of yours."

Tevy, the wolf, padded up to Rianthe and licked her cheek before tearing out in search of his brothers and sister.

Rianthe was still chuckling when she joined Kaiden and Roulf, ready to do her part to make camp for the night. While she set out snares, something stroked the hairs on the back of her neck. She whirled around to nothing but darkness. Still, an awareness that something was off-kilter grew within her. Eyes watched them, though she could not find them in the darkness. She returned to camp, intending to warn everyone to be mindful. As she moved past the trees into the clearing, the prescience hit her again. Rianthe whipped her sword from its scabbard and turned to the threat. Someone clothed in darkness advanced on her.

"Attackers," she yelled, her sword clanging against the weapon of the man who rushed her. "Protect yourselves!" *Tevy. Hide.* She had no time for a longer message before the man reset his blade and swooshed in low. Rianthe stopped his sword again, pushing back, calling upon her magic to protect them and feeling the flush of adrenalin course through her.

She met each parry, each thrust, forcing the man back into the trees.

We come.

No, Tevy. Hide. You must hide. Fear paralyzed her. The distraction almost cost her everything. The attacker swung for her neck and she barely got her sword up in time to deflect it.

It was time to finish this. Rianthe shoved the man, forcing him to release his downward thrust. He stumbled. Rianthe's sword filled his belly before he could regain his footing. He crumbled to the ground with nothing but death filling his eyes.

Rianthe raced back into camp, now a whirlwind of activity. Kaiden fought two men, Roulf a third, and the wolves surrounded two more, a tan and gray one in the midst of the fray.

"Tevy!" Rianthe screamed as she sprinted to help, pulling one of the men away from the wolves. This one fought with a fierceness her first attacker had lacked. He came at her again and again, backing her toward the fire. Completely on the defensive, she couldn't find a way around the man's assault. Her legs grew warm from the encroaching fire.

A wolf howled in pain, adding to her panic and the fear that congealed in her stomach. She must get to Tevy. With a gulp, she did the only thing she could think of. She threw herself across the fire pit. Flames licked at her clothing. She rolled, praying that would be enough to tamp them down. Beyond the fire, she leaped back to standing.

The man, surprised by her maneuver, had not yet rounded the pit. Rianthe charged to meet him, using her momentum to drive her sword straight through the front of his neck. He stood for a long moment, gurgling, his bloody breaths bubbling around her sword, his eyes round in surprise. Then, he sank to his knees.

Rianthe yanked her sword from his neck and didn't wait to see him hit the ground. She sped back into the fray, to Tevy. She must save him. The man the wolves had surrounded lay in a heap on the ground unmoving. His gashes and ripped skin meant the wolves had done their job well. Tevy stood there unharmed, looking, even in wolf form, inordinately pleased with himself.

He is not hurt, Taschia mind-spoke. *Grog has a minor gash, that is all.*

Camp had grown eerily quiet. Kaiden's attackers lay dead, as did Roulf's. The only sound was the huffing of hard breath as they each tried to calm their racing hearts in the aftermath of the battle. Roulf sank to the ground.

"Are you hurt?" Rianthe asked.

"I'm all right, child." He waved his hand in dismissal. "Just too old for this kind of thing." His eyes gleamed, denying his statement. "Still, it was a fine battle."

Kaiden went to each of the men. He checked their palms. Each was branded with a familiar upward arrow, with a thorn embedded in its side.

"Taegar sent them?"

"They carry her mark."

"Then we've lost the element of surprise. Taegar knows we're coming for her." The weight of her words settled like a cold, wet blanket over them all. Dread saturated Rianthe better than any drenching rain. Their one advantage had vanished.

"Let's deal with these men and get camp settled," Kaiden said, coming to her side. "Then we can figure out our next move. One step at a time, eh?" The worry in his eyes belied the crooked smile he tried to show.

He knew the same thing Rianthe did. They were totally screwed.

CHAPTER FIVE

Later, after they'd cleared the dead from their camp and everyone had settled in for some rest, Rianthe sat watch in the moonlight, wondering what lay ahead, racking her brain for some kind of edge for the coming confrontation. She had to come up with a way to defeat Taegar without harm to their small group.

She clutched at the bag around her neck. Their task seemed insurmountable, but Taegar must not remain in control of Origin cave. She must be stopped or everything they'd worked for, any chance they had for a future, would be lost.

"You worried, Ri?" Tevy asked, sitting up in his bedroll nearby. He shivered against the cold. Rianthe got up and wrapped her own cloak around him.

"Yes. And I'm worried about you. You shouldn't have come on this foolhardy quest."

"I'm a Royan, just like you, sister. I need to be here."

"You're too young for this."

Tevy laughed. "And you're old enough? What is old enough, anyhow? This is a brave new world and we all have to do our part."

"I just – I can't lose you. I'd die if something happened to you." Rianthe scrunched her face. Wrong phrase to use.

"Something already has happened. I've changed. I came into my True-Named abilities early. I can help."

When her own True-Naming had disappointed her, Rianthe had given up any pretense about the *awen* and her connection to it. Now, that rash decision might be the difference between success and failure. She'd lost so much time.

Tevy seemed to know what she was thinking. "You'll have what you need when the time comes."

"You can't know that, Tevy. I'm afraid...I'll let everyone down. I'll draw on the magic and nothing will happen except a rock rising from the ground. If that happens, the consequences will be dire." She whispered the words, afraid even to put a voice to them.

Her brother didn't hesitate in his response. "You'll have what you need when you need it. You always have. I've said it before, but I'll keep saying it until you trust yourself. I believe in you."

Therein lay the problem. Everyone believed in Rianthe except Rianthe. She hugged Tevy tight, murmuring a simple thank you. Her grip on the bag of runes tightened. They must not fall into Taegar's hands. Rianthe had chosen not to leave them home. If the opportunity arose to make the talisman whole again and use it to amplify their powers in the fight against Taegar, she needed to have them along. She glanced at Tevy. She recognized that since she would be front and center in this battle, having the remains of the talisman around her neck might not be the best idea.

She lifted the bag over her head and placed it around Tevy's neck. He pushed the bag away, trying to stop her.

"You must keep them, little brother. You'll be the most protected."

He will, Taschia agreed.

"But you might need them."

"They're useless until they're joined with the rest of the talisman. Until that time, it's good enough if they're nearby. And we can't risk these falling into the hands of our enemy."

Tevy clutched the bag tight. "All right. I understand. But you don't get to give up, okay?"

"What do you mean?" She yanked a veil of non-emotion over her face, stilled her features, and forced herself to remain outwardly calm. He couldn't know.

"I mean, it's like you're getting everything in place for when you're not here any longer. I don't want to lose you, either. You have to fight."

"I will fight. We can't see this battle's outcome, though, so it's smart to plan for every result."

"It may be smart, but that can't be our focus. You will win, Sister. I feel it in my soul."

Rianthe smiled at his formal name for her. "Uja always called me that. Sister."

Tevy nodded.

"I still miss him terribly."

"So do I." A brief sadness touched her brother's face before he kissed her goodnight and rolled in his bedroll to hunker down for the night, her cloak wound around his body as he went to sleep.

Rianthe stared out into the darkness, deep in thought. Did Tevy have prescient abilities? What did he sense? Rianthe wanted to buy into the hope he offered but she couldn't. She knew something no one else did. Something from her visions that only she had seen.

She would die in this battle. There was no other way to interpret what she'd seen. She'd never get the chance to do the things she'd dreamed about. Never get to explore a life with Kaiden in the absence of mortal danger. She wouldn't see Tevy grow up. She hung her head. So be it. If she gave them the hope of a future, it would be worth this final sacrifice.

Rianthe checked on Tevy, so angelic in sleep. So young. Without his wolf senses, he didn't stir when she knelt next to him. She tugged the cloak tighter around his shoulders and bent down, kissing his forehead as she smoothed his hair.

"I love you, little brother," she whispered. "Be safe. Please, please, be safe."

~~~

Two nights later, they arrived at the edge of the area surrounding Origin cave. There would be no fire tonight. They were too close. Everyone's mood, like the night, was dark, and they conversed in whispers. No one wanted to tempt fate, not this close to where Taegar waited.

For them.

The Dark druid knew they were coming. Based on the henchmen she'd already sent, she was ready to take them on. Readier than they were, a rag-tag group of wolves, warriors, and magicians with little actual power to call upon.

They had to succeed or everything would be lost. Earth would succumb to a greater power, and humankind
~~~

would be enslaved by darkness. If anyone lived, that is. The way things were going, Earth wouldn't be able to sustain life for much longer.

Which was the reason tomorrow demanded her sacrifice. Rianthe knew that. She would gladly die if it meant Tevy, Kaiden, New Hope, and all that is good in the world would continue.

What would it be like, to die? Would she go through immeasurable pain or would it be quick and silent? She would handle any pain if it left hope behind for the others. At least, she would try. Back in that first battle, when Deakon made her believe she was on fire, the agony had almost consumed her.

"A carrot for your thoughts."

Rianthe jumped at Kaiden's words. "Don't scare me like that."

Kaiden chuckled at the irony. "On a normal day, scaring you is impossible."

"I was...deep in thought."

"Obviously." He sat down next to her and leaned back against the same tree. "What about?"

Rianthe shrugged. She had no plans to tell Kaiden what she expected to happen tomorrow. "Just looking at this from all sides to be certain we've considered every angle."

"Being prepared is always good, though there's not much more we can do in terms of readiness."

"Do you have a good idea of the cave structure? Want to go over it again?"

"You and Roulf were clear in your descriptions. One main cave, several small alcoves, and two tunnels." He pointed as he spoke, a perfect description of the layout.

And the most amazing crystalline sparkles that

offered enough light to see. The hidden grotto had been covered in them. She'd never seen anything so beautiful, and she hoped it remained that way, and her parent's book lay hidden and still intact. Now was not the time to tell Kaiden all that, so Rianthe simply nodded. "More than likely, Taegar will be down one of those tunnels. But we can't rule out danger in any corner of that cave. We know from that battle in Minnie Apples that she has the ability to subvert people and call them to aid her."

"Agreed. We have to clear the alcoves before the tunnels."

"Maybe," Roulf said as he joined them, "Taegar will come out to meet us."

"Daylight is not Taegar's friend. She won't come out of the cave. She'll make us come to her."

"Then we'll enter her lair and adapt as the situation forces us to," Kaiden said. "Maybe we'll get lucky."

"Luck has not been our friend in battle so far."

They all nodded their heads as worry settled around them like a scratchy wool cloak. There was nothing else to say. Tomorrow would unfold as it would.

"I'll take watch. Try to sleep," Roulf said. "You both need it." He walked off into the darkness. Soon, they heard him settling against a tree.

Kaiden and Rianthe stared into the night. Finally, Rianthe stood. "I'm going to close my eyes for a while." Though she knew there would be no sleep this night.

"I should too." Kaiden stood next to her, then wrapped a tendril of her hair around his finger. "I'm glad you've grown your hair out."

When he tugged her hair, a tingle of contentedness filled her. The old days, when this had been so natural between them, seemed closer. They seemed closer.

"Kaiden?"

"Hmmm?"

"Would you stay? Tonight. With me. Like, well..."

Kaiden pulled her into his arms and hugged her tight. "It would be my honor."

They set their bedrolls beside each other and folded together, with Kaiden behind Rianthe, warming her back. She'd missed this so much. Missed their closeness and the rush of love that filled her in these rare moments. She wished she could remove her gloves and hold his hand, feel the texture of his skin.

"Thank you," she said.

"Trust me. It's my pleasure." His voice was rich and warm and, for this moment, free of stress and caution.

Rianthe snuggled into him, drawing in his woodsy scent. This was what she missed. So much. Now, on the eve of a battle that would decide their futures, she ached with the bittersweet memories of their early days. Kaiden had been her champion from the day she'd fallen into his arms at the age of ten. A man always at war with his sense of duty, he'd made the tough choice between protecting her or protecting the future of New Hope and the world. He was filled with love deeper than anyone knew. Rianthe held her grieving heart inside with a fist to her chest. To have found this again...now...when destiny allowed no future for them. No future for her. Her thoughts were poisoned daggers slaughtering any remaining tendril of peace.

"It's all right, Ri." Kaiden's sleepy whisper warmed her ear. "Sleep now. You're safe." He tightened his arm around her for a moment. "I've got you."

Rianthe closed her eyes tight against the sting of tears. With her own gloved hand, she rubbed his hand that lay across her belly. Her strong man. Her protector. She tried to picture Kaiden living without her. Finding happiness with someone else. She wanted to be happy for him. Really, she did.

No. Rianthe opened her eyes and willed the tears away. She refused to contemplate those possibilities. That only increased the ache in her heart. Instead, she turned to watch Tevy, his chest rising and falling in the deep sleep of a twelve-year-old. Rianthe imagined him as a man, a great wolf. Bonding with a mate, having children. She imagined Fraka, too, with her nephew, Ujami. His father, Uja, would never see his son grown up. Neither would Rianthe, though because of Ujami's magic—his ability to coax sustenance from the soil, just like his father—humankind would thrive.

All they had to do was destroy the most powerful druid in the world.

Rianthe tried to sleep and lost part of her night to dreams. In the early hours, she slipped out of Kaiden's arms with regret and went to the edge of their little camp. Sitting down facing east, she watched the dawn bring light to the new day.

She let her tears fall, just for that moment.

"Thank you," she whispered to the air, the sky, the trees, and the ground. She pulled off her gloves and touched the dirt beneath her. No vision came, no reckoning. Only silence. "Thank you," she said to Earth. "For the life you gave me. I don't regret any of it."

A sigh reached her, a short-lived, small breath of air. Her hand warmed. The warmth traveled up her arm, through her chest then engulfed her entire body. A warmth that spoke of tenderness, friendship, and healing love. Everything good about life swelled within her as time slowed, and nothing remained but her and Earth. One entity. One being. One focus: searching out the way for Earth and humanity to co-exist and thrive.

"I will do everything in my power to ensure your survival. And...I wish you happiness. Health. Peace. I wish all that for you."

Wet tears melded with the smile on her face. She didn't wipe them away until she heard the stirrings in the camp behind her. Reluctantly, Rianthe pulled her hand away and slipped her glove back on.

Goodbye, she whispered.

~~~

They moved in silence through the woods surrounding Origin cave, each working their way to pre-designated spots. Rianthe, Kaiden, and Taschia waited under cover of the trees, giving the others time to get in position before they made their move.

Tevy could see where they waited. His eyesight was much stronger in wolf form. Everything was stronger. Rianthe had hugged him hard one last time before they'd split up. He'd wanted to tell her why he was sad. He'd seen a dire sense about today in her eyes, but that would have only diverted her attention and worsened the situation. And it was only a feeling. It wasn't like he knew anything tangible. He didn't have visions like Rianthe. He only got...a sense of things.

We are ready, Hark mind-spoke to him. *Our sister says it is almost time.*

Energy thrummed through his brother wolves, exhilaration barely contained. Tevy embraced it himself, pushing away the worry. Now was not the time. Now...it was time for the hunt.
~~~

CHAPTER SIX

Rianthe pulled her gloves off and glanced at Kaiden. Roulf had given him another stealth rock, like he'd used to make them almost invisible when they'd taken Deakon down. Kaiden murmured the words Roulf taught him, then signaled for Rianthe and Taschia to stay close as they moved into the clearing, following the tree line as far as they could for cover. With no trees near the cave, though, they eventually had to leave their shelter behind and step unprotected into the open area in front of the cave entrance. It surprised Rianthe that no magic hid the opening this time, but it shouldn't have, considering Taegar had taken control of the place. Not for long, if Rianthe and company had anything to do with it.

With her heart racing, Rianthe cautioned herself to expect the unexpected. Taegar was too powerful to let a little covert cave-hiding magic slow her down. She would have been impatient for the power within. Power she now controlled. Rianthe shook her head to clear those thoughts and focus on the here and now.

Still crouching, they snuck closer. They could only pray that Roulf's rock hid them until there were close enough.

No such luck. Six men filed out of the cave. All wore the cloak of the Dark circle. The ruse was up. They'd been discovered.

"Taegar knows all," the man in the center intoned. "Taegar knew you would come."

Rianthe straightened first, drawing her sword. She needed to get in front of Kaiden, to protect him.

Kaiden, of course, would have none of it. He shoved her behind him, going completely against what they'd planned. Stepping to his side, Rianthe stared at him for a long moment, daring him to argue with her stance.

He didn't. Smart man. He drew his sword and kept his eyes on the immediate danger.

Now they could focus on the real threat. "We are not here for you," Rianthe told them. "We have come for the druid."

"You will not succeed. She offers you this. Surrender. Join with us. Your magic will be limitless, your lives never-ending."

In a crouch, Rianthe steeled herself. She picked up a fistful of dirt. No vision hit her, only a shiver, a sense of something filling her soul. She stared at the men. "Your plan would be at the expense of Earth and everyone who lives upon it, including yourselves. No thank you. We renounce your offer."

"Then you shall die this day." The man raised his arm and white light shot toward Rianthe.

She swung her sword up just in time to deflect the

bolt. And the next, and the next. One after another, light shot from each of the six. Rianthe glanced at Kaiden. Whatever power he had protected him well, as his sword moved this way and that, deflecting the magic thrown at them.

Taegar's acolytes moved closer and, as one, Rianthe and Kaiden stepped forward. Taschia held back. Just like in the Fringes, she served as the perimeter fighter while Rianthe took the central focus.

You cannot escape.

The words filled her mind, not one voice, but six, speaking as one. Sounds, like a rushing waterfall, filled her ears until she couldn't hear anything else. Kaiden clapped his hand over one ear, so hers wasn't the only mind invaded by these sounds.

A ploy meant to distract them. That's what this was. Rianthe tried to shut out the din, to focus on the battle at hand. Her prescience helped her turn just in time to deflect fire from her left. A wolf, Marin, leaped from the bushes and bit into the man's arm. He screamed, his fire disappearing. Grog joined Marin, and they wrestled the man to the ground, pulling him back into the trees.

One down.

Rianthe focused on the remaining men. Kaiden stood ahead of her, holding off all the firepower directed their way. She caught up, her sword joining his. "I'll stay on defense," he said. "Try to get a hit in like you did against Marta. You can do it."

She focused, bringing her own fire to the fore and lashing out. It caught the central man, then spread, hitting all five robed men, surrounding them in sizzling lightning streaks. She'd done it! Kaiden's wry grin said he'd noticed, too. Except, the men should have caught fire, but they didn't. Instead, the sparks rolled off them as if they'd hit some sort of shield.

Rianthe's magic was finite. There was no guessing how long it would aid her, so she made each hit count. This time, instead of a full-on attack, she threw a sizzling bolt at the ground in front of the men. When it hit with a thunk of searing fire, it did little damage but the man closest jumped. She tossed another scorching bolt, this time hitting that man's chest. It caught him unaware and pierced whatever shield protected him. In a fizzle of burning, stinking flesh, he died.

Kaiden grinned at her. Two down, four to go.

The remaining men split up. They spread apart to make it harder to target them. One of their fireballs streaked past Kaiden, leaving a bloody tear along his arm, yet his sword never once dipped.

Rianthe tried the same tactic with the next dark-robe, but he side-stepped and maintained his barrage on her and Kaiden. Still, she had a plan. Distraction, then a death hit.

I need distractions. One at a time, she mind-spoke to Taschia.

We come.

Her sister-wolf leaped from the cover of the trees onto the back of one of the robed men. Rianthe threw an inferno toward him, and Taschia jumped away as the fire hit its mark. The man went down in another writhing, burning pile of foul-smelling flesh.

Are you all right?

I am unharmed, Taschia replied. *This is fun.*

Rianthe barely had time to shake her head. The three remaining men intensified their attack, heading straight for Rianthe and Kaiden while they threw bolt after bolt.

The noise in her head worsened until Rianthe thought she might burst apart.

"It's time to finish this," she shouted to Kaiden.

He nodded, sweating with the effort it took him to deflect their fire weapons.

As one unit, they advanced. While the wolves distracted the dark-robes, Rianthe fired and Kaiden protected. Neither sword touched flesh. This battle began with magic and ended the same way.

When it was over, it seemed like hours had passed yet the sun hadn't shifted much in the sky. Rianthe looked around at the bedraggled group of heroes, panting and tired, a sense of accomplishment wiping away her own exhaustion. Tevy sat on his haunches with the other wolves, tongue lolling out the side of his mouth, a wide wolf-smile showing dangerous canines.

"We did it," Rianthe said, hearing the wonder in her own voice. "We really did it."

"Of course you did," Roulf said, applying a bandage to Kaiden's arm. The little man had stayed back as their last resort weapon. "I knew you would win."

"Well, I didn't," she said.

"I didn't have time to think about it," Kaiden said.

"And this was only the first volley."

Roulf nodded. "We must press our advantage before the Dark druid has time to regroup."

Rianthe would have preferred to wait. Kaiden looked pale, but otherwise all right as he flexed his arm.

"I'm fine," Kaiden said with a grin. "Just a sting, nothing more. I'm ready."

My brothers and I are ready too. We want to hunt more, Taschia mind-spoke.

They all stared at the entrance to Origin cave.

Nothing showed but darkness. Not even a hint of the light stream Rianthe knew was inside. That surprised her. The entrance should be glowing, some inkling that the energy still flowed. She didn't notice the jangled discordance either, the feeling that had plagued her during her training here with Roulf.

She felt nothing. Except death.

CHAPTER SEVEN

Rianthe crouched down to rest, staring at the dead. None of them had turned to ash. If her belief was correct, that meant they had not followed the druid way, but rather were unnaturally infused with magic by Taegar.

Taegar.

Thus far, the Dark druid had been quiet, letting her acolytes fight to the death for her. Rianthe stood and stared at the cave entrance. Taegar must be inside. Somewhere. Rianthe tensed, knowing that soon they would take on the enemy who'd brought so much misery upon them. Soon, they would be face-to-face with the druid who must pay for her sins.

Kaiden joined her after he helped the wolves drag the carcasses away from the clearing. Roulf flanked Rianthe on the other side, and all five wolves stood behind them ready for the next fight.

"How is your energy, child?" Roulf asked.

Rianthe felt pumped and that surprised her. Her body thrummed with leftovers of the *awen* coursing through her. For the first time since she'd found her ability, she was stronger afterwards than she'd been before using magic.

The real test was yet to come. This was the most difficult thing she'd ever done, to stand here with the knowledge that she would face her destiny in this tunnel.

Rianthe glanced up at the sky one last time, giving in briefly to her grief over an event that hadn't even happened yet. This fatalistic attitude of hers wasn't the best way to start this battle. Maybe it wouldn't happen the way the *ehwaz* had shown her.

Her vision had been pretty clear, though. And so far, each of her visions had proven to be true.

What happened to her was not important in the larger picture. They must retake Origin cave if Earth and those who lived upon it were to survive. If Tevy were to survive. And baby Ujami, Kaiden, and everyone else.

So be it. Rianthe picked up her sword and turned to the maw of the enemy. She might not come out of that cave again, but she would give Taegar the fight of her life. She'd need every bit of help she could get, so she stripped off her boots. Barefoot, she'd have direct contact with Earth, the source of all her magic.

The vision hit her so fast, she gasped. Rianthe saw inside Origin cave. The familiar walls, the glittering alcove where she'd found the book her parents had left for her, still secured behind the hidden wall. She saw everything.

The magic still flowed, a stream of light, yellow-tinged now, with an altar built up around it, the *awen* clearly weaker than before. Taegar's doing, most likely.

Rianthe sensed a sadness, one she recognized. Earth had weakened along with the light. They were running out of time.

Rianthe looked around the large cavern. Taegar was not there.

I am waiting for you, little one. Come to me.

Though the words were only in her head, Rianthe shivered. Even knowing what she did about the Dark druid, the wraith's siren song resonated in Rianthe's blood. With a tough-fought focus, Rianthe saw that the two entrances leading deeper into the cave system were unguarded. As hard as she tried to divine down which tunnel Taegar waited, she could not. No, wait, there, to the left. Something lay down that tunnel. A force, a darkness.

Taegar.

Closing off the vision, Rianthe looked at Kaiden and Roulf. "She's in there."

"Where?" Kaiden asked, eyeing the opening.

"Not in the main chamber. She's down one of the tunnels. I can't tell which one." She lied. With a glance at the wolves, she closed her mind so her purpose would remain hers alone.

Roulf scrutinized her for a few seconds, then nodded. "We may not know until we get in there."

"Or even then. We'll have to split up," Kaiden said.

The wolves, Tevy among them, all whined, causing the three people to turn and look at them.

Hark said splitting our pack is not good, Taschia mind-spoke.

"Unless you have a better plan, it's the only way. If one of us finds Taegar, we can call the others to join us," Rianthe said, keeping her voice calm so no hint of her true plan emerged.

Hark whined again, but dropped his head briefly, acknowledging that the wolves would follow the plan. Kaiden waved at the cave entrance. "Rianthe, Tevy, and I will take one tunnel. Roulf, you and the remaining wolves take the other.

Rianthe shook her head. She didn't want Tevy to witness her death and be plagued by the memories for the rest of his life. "Tevy should stay with the pack so they can protect him."

Tevy whined. *I am not a child.*

Yes, you are.

"I disagree," Kaiden said. "We can keep a better eye on him if he's with us."

I am a wolf. I can fight.

"No." She would stand firm on this. The only way to protect Tevy, and the runes that hung around his neck, lay in keeping him away from her. Tevy must not be at her side when she found Taegar. "He goes with the wolves or we don't do this."

Kaiden stared at her long and hard. She wasn't telling him everything and he knew it. He'd just have to deal. This was something she couldn't, wouldn't tell anyone. He wanted to argue with her. The deep furrow in his forehead told her that. Instead, he held his silence, surprising her. He gave her a curt nod.

He was thinking they'd have this out later. If only she could tell him. She longed to be able to talk about everything with him as they had before. To have a future they shared.

I stay with you, Taschia said.

"No. You must tell me if Taegar is down the other tunnel." *And I need you to keep Tevy safe.*

You are hiding something.

Rianthe looked away. Taschia, her best friend and sister-wolf, knew her too well. "Don't engage Taegar if you determine her whereabouts," Rianthe said to Hark. "Call for us." She took a deep breath. "All right, let's go." In the lead, she walked into the cave. The uneven, rock-filled ground made her miss her boots.

Inside, the discordant resonance that had plagued her during her training was present, even amplified. A sourness filled the air. The sparkling walls were now dark and suppressed. Origin cave did not like the changes occurring. That much was obvious. And the light...

Roulf glanced her way. He knew what she'd already discerned. The light had dimmed. A lot. Rianthe wished that light could improve her own magic but so far, that had not been the answer to unlocking her abilities.

The soils of Earth would be her enhancer. The dark earth lay cold beneath her feet, a chill that infiltrated her and caused her to shiver. Uneven clods of dirt made her step with care as she moved around the altar to look down the two tunnels.

"I get no sense which one to take," Roulf said.

Rianthe nodded to the left one. "Kaiden and I will take this one. You and the wolves take the other."

Kaiden and Roulf nodded. The wolves moved to the other tunnel. Rianthe went to Tevy. She ran her hand along his fur, wanting to say so much to him. *You take care of yourself, brother.*

Always. He cocked his head as she hugged him. *Are you all right?*

"I'm fine," Rianthe said, swiping at her cheek. "I love you, and I don't want anything to happen to you. Ever."

I love you, too. I will take care of myself. His blue wolf-eyes focused on her. *Will you take care of yourself?*

Rianthe smiled, or tried to. She pressed her hand to the pouch around her wolf-brother's neck. *Take care of this, too.*

Today, she would regain the rest of the talisman, or die trying. Every ounce of strength Rianthe owned would be given to that endeavor. She would give it all so Tevy would remain safe.

JUDGMENT

CHAPTER EIGHT

Small nooks peppered the sides of the tunnel, some large enough to stand in, some nothing more than pockmarks in the granite. Movement by feel became impossible, so Rianthe uncovered a glow to help them. During their previous visit, Rianthe and Roulf had only searched partway down these tunnels, which meant she soon stepped in unfamiliar territory. She'd caught Kaiden off guard by heading into the left tunnel without notice and now it wasn't wide enough for him to take lead. Rianthe should be in front anyway. This was her problem to solve.

I wait for you.

The voice filled her head, grating against every nerve. Rianthe glanced at Kaiden, who remained focused on their immediate surroundings. He hadn't heard. This voice, Taegar's voice, was meant only for her.

And I'm coming to end this, once and for all, Rianthe

answered.

The laughter that echoed back spiked through Rianthe's brain, harsh and discordant.

"What are you doing, Ri? What do you sense?" Kaiden whispered.

She'd slowed, almost to a complete stop, without realizing it. Rianthe blew out a breath, wondering how she would keep her wits about her, keep Kaiden safe, keep Tevy from joining them, take back the talisman, and destroy Taegar. All before she returned to Earth in ashen form, joining her parents in the afterlife.

"We picked the correct tunnel," she told Kaiden. "She's ahead." At least Tevy would be safe.

"How do you know?"

"Because I hear her. In my head. She knows we're coming."

"Are we...are you...ready?"

Rianthe shrugged in the near darkness. "As ready as I can be. I guess we'll soon find out if I'm strong enough."

"You sound almost defeated, Ri. Like you've already lost the battle."

"Haven't I? My entire life has been in preparation for this moment, yet I'm an infant when it comes to tapping into the *awen*."

Kaiden's hand settled on her shoulder and he squeezed. "You can't go into battle thinking you'll lose or you will."

Though danger lurked ahead of them, Rianthe smiled. She'd heard that authoritarian tone of voice on the Training fields many, many times, except now the tinge of concern edged out the worst of his dictatorial coaching.

"You recognize your disadvantages," Kaiden continued. "And you look for ways to overcome them. Battles constantly change. Search for the enemy's weaknesses, but don't give in to them unless you're certain they're not a ruse. Above all, remember to use your own strengths."

She would utilize every bit of training Kaiden had pushed her through. But... "I'm grateful to you, Kaiden. For everything. The training, your friendship, all of it. I would never have made it this far without you."

Kaiden shifted, stopping inches from her. "Don't you give up on me, Ri. We'll make it through this. There's too much still to do, too many adventures yet to live." Intense green eyes stared down at her, daring her to look away. Then, before she could blink or think, Kaiden kissed her. A quick, hard, wonderful kiss. Rianthe dug her toes into the dirt to anchor herself as the connection between them flared. All the wonderful parts of him flowed through her during that short kiss and the darkness she'd felt before all but disappeared.

Kaiden stared at her. Had he seen her truth?

"Now you kiss me?" she asked, easing the furrow between his eyes with her fingers.

His swift grin lightened her heart. Touched with anxiety, it reminded her what they fought for. Rianthe had always loved his smile.

"I need you to remember why you want to stick around," Kaiden said. He squeezed her shoulder again. "I need you to fight."

"I will," she said. Right up until the end. "I always planned to." Rianthe peered down the tunnel. A pinprick of light at the other end called them forward. That was where they would finally come face-to-face with Taegar.

Where the epic battle she'd been warned about her entire life would come to pass.

This would be her last stand.

~~~

Something was off. Kaiden didn't understand what, but the finality in Rianthe's words concerned him, almost more than what lay ahead. Rianthe the fighter, he knew how to handle. Here, now, with this fatalistic attitude, she scared him more than Taegar.

Sorting it out would have to wait, since Rianthe moved ahead, her footsteps and stance resolute. The time for battle had come.

The pinprick of light in front of them grew as they neared. Unlike the warmth of sunlight, this looked unnatural. A cold, stark, yellowed glow. Just before they breached the entranceway to the cavern that held the light, Rianthe turned to him. "I love you, Kaiden."

Words he'd wanted to hear, to say, for so many years. That she would say them now only added to his sense of foreboding. Rianthe gave him no chance to worry as she forged ahead into the chamber. Kaiden's heart thudded in his chest as it hit him. Rianthe would do whatever she must to prevail this day even if it meant giving her life.

That. Would. Not. Happen. This last thought hung in Kaiden's mind as he joined Rianthe and prepared himself to do whatever he could. His focus might differ from hers, but they were both ready to sacrifice everything for their cause.

Kaiden would do it to keep Rianthe alive.

They would both live through this. They must.

"Here you are," a voice said, pulling his thoughts. "You have finally come to me."
~~~

Taegar stood on the far side of the chamber. Not really stood, more like floated. She bobbed up and down, more ghost-like than human. A golden aura surrounded the long, dark robe that hung straight from her shoulders, offering little definition to her shapelessness.

She raised her head, giving Kaiden his first face-to-face look into her golden eyes. Eyes in a formless face. Nothing but black fog surrounded them. What was she?

He glanced at Rianthe, who barely blinked. Her eyes remained on Taegar, fierce with emotion. Anger, pain, fear. All appeared to course through her, just as it did through him.

"We have found you," Rianthe ground out.

Taegar cocked her hooded head. "I have led you here. You would not have known I'd found your little secret unless I wanted you to."

"You forget," Ri said, her tone flat. "I have bested you."

"In the *ehwaz*? In visions? Ha!" The Dark druid's discordant laugh made Kaiden vibrate like he stood on a precipice in a strong wind. It tried to sway him, to push him over the side. That voice. He would fall.

Rianthe's hand settled on his clothed arm, grounding him. Bringing him back from the edge. "Focus on me," she said.

Kaiden nodded, worried that he'd almost succumbed to Taegar. How could they defeat her?

"Isn't that sweet," Taegar said. "True love wins the day."

Rianthe kept her counsel. She seemed worried, but stood strong and resolute. Anger and hatred didn't seem to be coloring her choices. That bode well.

"You will not win the final battle," Taegar

continued.

Rianthe tilted her head, again keeping her silence.

Taegar focused on Rianthe. She seemed to have dismissed Kaiden from her mind. This battle would be between these two formidable beings. As an outsider, the only action left to Kaiden was to pray that his calling aided him when needed so he could keep Rianthe alive.

"I gave you chance after chance to join me," Taegar said. "You have no idea of the power I can grant you. Limitless power."

Rianthe barked a laugh. "Power doled out by you at the cost of so many."

"Insignificant."

"Only to you." Rianthe hadn't moved a muscle since she'd first responded to Taegar.

"They should be to you, too, little one." Taegar pointed a bony finger at her. "You are more than they are. You are the new evolution. Like me. You are meant to survive in the new world we will create."

"A world devoid of humanity. Of earthen sustenance."

"We thrive on power, you and I. Not field greens. We will have no need for food grown from the soil."

"There is every need."

"This is getting us nowhere." Taegar straightened, or maybe she floated higher above the ground. Either way, she grew. She filled her end of the cave, loomed over them. Rianthe didn't flinch. She stayed focused on the apparition in front of her, unwavering.

Taegar's bony hand reached beneath her robes and came out with a handful of something Kaiden couldn't see well. Stones?

Rianthe took a step forward, her eyes fixated on

Taegar's hand. Kaiden strained his eyes to see in the gloom. Not stones. Runes. The runes he'd lost to Deakon.

"Where are the remaining runes, little one? I will have them." Taegar's voice grew the same as her ghostly body. It boomed throughout the cave, bouncing off the chamber walls until Kaiden wanted to cover his ears.

Rianthe stood immobile. "You will never get them," she said, her voice eerily calm.

Taegar glided forward and Kaiden shifted his weight, bracing his sword. Taegar's finger flicked in his direction. Through no plan of his own, he was frozen, unable to move. He struggled against the invisible shield. Not even a finger budged no matter how hard he tried. Nothing. His worst nightmare. He could see everything, but was powerless to interact. He was *thurisaz*, but no longer able to protect.

Panic choked him. Rianthe was on her own, and she could not defeat Taegar like that. She needed him. Needed his touch to flare her magic, just like it had back in Minor Town.

He fought to reach out. He needed to touch her, but he couldn't. "Grab my hand," he said, or tried to. No sound came from his lips. Fear he'd rarely known before rushed in. He was True-Named protector, and he stood there, frozen and tormented, helpless to prevent what would unfold.

"I will have them," Taegar said. Light shot from her hand.

Rianthe raised her sword and Taegar's lightning arrow bounced off. It must have been strong because Rianthe backed up a step. At least she was mobile. An inkling of hope touched Kaiden.

Fire-arrow after fire-arrow shot at Rianthe while

Kaiden struggled to break Taegar's grip. Rianthe held her ground, but each blast rocked her, giving her no time to gather her energy and fight back. Dram, but he needed to free himself. To help her.

"I am *tiwaz*, ruler of all. Stronger than anyone. You cannot best me," Taegar said.

Rianthe grunted. She couldn't fight and talk at the same time. Beads of sweat formed on her forehead as she tried to hold off the Dark druid.

Several long minutes passed, filled with Taegar's never-ending barrage of fire. Then, suddenly, it all stopped. Taegar lowered her arms.

Rianthe didn't let up on her defensive posture and hadn't yet returned the attack, though fear dilated her eyes. Cunning, too. She watched, learned, just as Kaiden had taught her, saving her energy until she formulated a plan.

Stuck in place, all he could do was hope he'd taught her enough.

CHAPTER NINE

Fear all but paralyzed Rianthe. To fight back was impossible. It took all her strength to fend off Taegar's attacks, and this wasn't the worst the druid could do.

Kaiden remained immobile and silent beside her. Probably Taegar's doing. The stark fear and determination in his wide eyes told her something kept him from helping her no matter how hard he struggled.

"Where would you put the talisman?" Taegar mused. "I do not see the telltale bulge under your clothing, little one. Do you even have it on you?"

The possibility that Taegar would search out the runes scared Rianthe more than anything. If she found Tevy... No. Rianthe cleared her mind. The Dark druid must not find the runes. That could not happen. She must keep Taegar's focus on her. Rianthe kept her sword in front of her and took a step forward.

"I will never let the talisman fall into your hands."

Taegar didn't take the bait. "I think you've handed them off rather than bring them so close to their rightful owner. But to whom?" She laughed suddenly. "I've got it. That whelp of a brother."

It took every ounce of Rianthe's control to obscure the staggering terror that flash-froze her heart. Taegar must not get to Tevy. Rianthe would not allow it.

"Yessss," Taegar said with a snake's hiss. "And he's here, isn't he? Nearby. Ohhh, this is sweet nectar. I will have the talisman to bind Earth's magic to me forever. I will destroy you and your brother. My nemesis will be no more, and no one else is even minimally able to defeat me. The Royan lineage ends here and now."

We see you, Taschia mind-spoke. *You are with the dark one. We come to help.*

No! Stay. You must.

We come to help.

No. She didn't want Tevy there. The danger was too great.

But he was coming, and she couldn't stop him from getting hurt, or worse. Except by making it safer.

The calm front Rianthe had tried to project disappeared. Everything inside her came crashing out. All the anger, hatred, and fear poured forth. She let it all go, threw it away to make room for the magic. Closing her eyes for a scarce second, the discordant sound of Earth's *awen* called to her. The soil beneath her feet hummed.

Her power swelled. This was the time to meet her destiny. She was *sowilo*, the prophesied one. Rianthe opened her eyes and stared at Taegar's fluid form. "You will die. Now," Rianthe screamed.

Magic whooshed out from her, translucent and deadly. It held no fire, only frigid, raw power. The wave caught Taegar unaware and she stumbled back under the onslaught.

Rianthe pressed her advantage, sending wave after glacial wave against her enemy.

Eyes glowing brightly with her attempt to thwart Rianthe, Taegar jerked back until the cave wall stopped her. The wall itself turned blue-white with ice. Taegar's golden eyes were large and round with shock at Rianthe's strength.

The energy drain staggered Rianthe. She gave every part of herself to send this power forth. If she kept going it would kill her, yet still, she pushed the power out, held Taegar to the frozen rock. Ferocious in her effort to destroy the Dark druid before she got to Tevy, Rianthe pushed forward as her pure energy streamed toward Taegar. This. Would. End. Now.

Even as she had the thought, weakness consumed her. She couldn't keep this up, even with Earth's help. If Taegar didn't give way soon, all would be lost.

Rianthe noticed movement in her peripheral vision. Could it be?

Yes! Kaiden was free. He charged to help her. He touched her, his hand settling on the back of her neck, adding warmth to the chill that suffused her. He gave her his strength. His magic bolstered her own, allowed her to keep the wall of frigid power strong, never wavering, never stopping. She gave everything she had, just as the prophecy said she would.

We are almost there. Do not give all of yourself. Please.

Rianthe heard Tevy's words, but she did not dare stop. Power consumed her. Hatred for this entity who had caused them all so much pain. Fear for Tevy. It must end.

Taegar must die. She narrowed her focus. It was just her and Taegar, the Dark druid who'd all but destroyed New Hope. Who'd killed Uja as surely as if she'd held the sword herself. Who'd taken Bhren from them before Rianthe had finished her studies.

Taegar, who'd killed Rianthe's parents.

Who'd destroyed every bit of happiness in Rianthe's life.

She. Must. Die.

Taegar wilted further into the wall, her eyes dimming.

Renewing her efforts, Rianthe strengthened the shield that held the druid back. Again and again, she threw layers of magic at the wall.

When Tevy and the wolves burst into the chamber, fear for her brother's safety distracted Rianthe. Just for a moment. Long enough for the druid to shoot a bolt of fire into the pack of wolves.

Rianthe screamed and threw whatever she had left within her at Taegar, trying hard not to draw too much of Kaiden's magic. The Dark druid's form became translucent. Rianthe kept pouring magic into the wavering form.

Kaiden stumbled, so Rianthe yanked his hand away. When he stepped closer, she held out her arm, her magic pushing him back, holding him as effectively as Taegar had. She would not let this battle use him up. Tears streamed down her face. *I'm sorry,* she mouthed. And she was. She refused to tell him how this would end. That she wouldn't be with him...after. She silently gave thanks that she'd told him how she felt about him. It had been her last chance.

Pushing all thoughts away, Rianthe focused on

Taegar. Nothing but a wisp of something ethereal remained, and that was only for a moment before it vanished completely, swallowed up by Rianthe's magic.

Rianthe let go of the power, let it fade away. She'd done it. She'd defeated the Dark druid and saved Earth, Tevy, Kaiden, and the rest of the world.

Good thing, too, because she had nothing left. The life ebbed out of her as she sank to the floor. She'd done what Roulf had warned her not to do. She'd let the magic use her up. To save Tevy, she'd had to embrace death, just as she'd seen in her vision.

So be it.

Rianthe saw, out of the corner of her eye, Kaiden rushing toward her. He would be too late.

She closed her eyes and gave herself up to destiny.

~~~

Everything happened at once. The wolves howled as a bolt of lightning hit them, Taegar disappeared, and Rianthe fell to the floor, unconscious. Kaiden didn't know which way to go.

"See to Rianthe," Roulf yelled. "I'll help the pack."

Kaiden dropped to Rianthe's side, Taschia beside him. She barely breathed and was as pale and cold as a winter moon. He checked her arms, legs, head. Nothing appeared broken and he didn't see her bleeding anywhere.

Taschia nudged Rianthe's arm, but it lay slack. With a deep keening whine, the wolf looked up at Kaiden.

I cannot sense my sister.

"Ri," he whispered, pulling her still, limp body to his chest. "Wake up, Ri. Please. You did it. You killed Taegar and saved us. You *saved* us. You have to wake up." Kaiden's heart sheared in two as he held her close.
~~~

Tears wet his cheeks. Hugging her tight, he willed his own energy into her body. He touched her skin, her arms, her hair, her cheek, searching for their connection. Nothing happened. Nothing changed. No, no, no, no. He couldn't lose her. Kaiden sat there on the ground, holding Rianthe, rocking back and forth and praying to Earth to bring her back to him.

Her skin was cold. Kaiden's hand on her chest told him she still breathed, but it was so shallow. And for how long? She'd fallen into this sleep for a reason and he had to find a way to bring her back.

He barely realized it when Roulf joined him. The little man placed a hand on Rianthe's cheek and bent near her for a long time. When he raised his head, his eyes were bleak. "She has gone deep within herself."

"What does that mean?" Kaiden cried.

Roulf was quiet for too long as he stared at Rianthe. When he spoke, his voice broke. "She may have given too much of herself. She let the magic use her up."

"Will she—" Kaiden stumbled over the word.

"Only time will tell." Roulf shook his head. He placed a hand on her cheek again. "She has to fight this battle on her own. We can only wait. Right now," he touched Kaiden's shoulder, "we need your help."

"I can't leave her. I won't."

"The wolves need help," Roulf said.

Kaiden's eyes widened. "Tevy?" If he'd been hit, or worse, there would be no recovering from this day. Kaiden turned his head, trying to find Tevy among the wolves crowding around something. He craned his head, searching through the semi-darkness of the cave. Panic filled him, rising up like bile in his throat, closing it off.

"Tevy is fine," Roulf said quickly, allaying this part

of Kaiden's worry. "A slight burn, nothing more. He will heal. Hark is injured."

Taschia whined.

Would this day's grief never end?

One of the wolves looked Kaiden's way, then began to shimmer.

Tevy, having shifted back to human form, dropped to the floor beside Kaiden, his hand settling on top of Kaiden's over Rianthe's heart. "Ri!"

"She lives," Roulf said, running his hand over the boy's hair. "That's all we can ask for the moment."

"She has to wake up. She just has to. She's all I have left."

Kaiden saw the tears in Tevy's eyes as he laid his head gently on his sister's chest.

He shared the boy's sentiment. He laid Rianthe's listless body gently on the ground and settled his cape under her head. "Stay with her while I check on Hark." Kaiden tipped Tevy's head up to look at him. "Talk to her, Tev. Hopefully, that will help her find her way back to us."

Tevy nodded, turning his focus back to his sister, his whispered words unintelligible to anyone but Rianthe.

"I wish I had healing abilities," Roulf whispered. "For both of them."

Hark lay on the ground, surrounded by his brothers and sister. Marin, Joek, and Grog all tried to give their warmth to their fallen brother and wouldn't move to let Kaiden and Roulf take a look.

Taschia? Kaiden mind-spoke, asking for some help.

Reluctantly, Grog stood and moved away. Kaiden finally got a look at the extent of Hark's injuries. The wolf was still unconscious.

"He's got a large gash on his hindquarters," Kaiden said.

Roulf placed his hand on the wolf's side.

He was thrown against the wall by the evil one's magic, Taschia said.

Hark let out a small whine. He lifted his head and his whine worsened.

"He's probably got a wolf-sized headache," Roulf said. "If I am sensing correctly, he's all right except for the headache and the wound."

All the wolves cried their relief, their howls echoing off the cavern walls. It wasn't enough to ease Kaiden's own pain and worry, but it helped just a bit.

Together, he and Roulf bound Hark's wounded leg. "He won't be able to walk back to New Hope," Roulf said.

"Neither will Ri," Kaiden added. "We'll need to build a sled."

"Two of them, most likely."

My brothers and I are strong. We will pull our brother and sister, Taschia said to Kaiden.

He nodded, looking around the chamber where so much pain had happened. "Let's move them to the outer chamber, then we can build fires for warmth while we build the sleds."

Kaiden carried Rianthe up the tunnel to the first cavern. She looked way too pale. "Wake up, Ri," he whispered, kissing her temple. "Please." Kaiden hadn't begged for much in his life, but he begged now. He couldn't lose her. Not now, when they'd begun to find each other again.

He settled her near the entrance to the cave, hoping daylight might help revive her. Tevy and Roulf stayed with Rianthe while he walked back down the tunnel to carry Hark, flanked by the wolves. He carefully laid Hark next to Rianthe. Hark's brothers, along with Taschia, settled around them both, adding their warmth. Tevy stayed in human form and sat at Rianthe's head, stroking her hair, talking to her in quiet bursts as he wiped at the tears that lined his face with muddy trails.

"Her breaths are even, but I can barely feel them," Tevy said.

"She breathes. That is the best we can hope for at the moment," Roulf said.

Kaiden knelt beside her. He took her hand, praying their connection would help her. "Wake up, Ri. Come back to us. Your family's waiting for you. I'm waiting for you." For interminable minutes, he watched for a reaction. A jerk, an eye-twitch, anything to give them a sign she heard them. She remained motionless, deep in a place beyond his reach.

Still as death.

I still do not sense my sister, Taschia mind-spoke. *She is a long, long way from us.*

Kaiden sighed. He glanced at Tevy for a moment, then back at Rianthe. "We're going to get her home. Home to heal. Home to show her how her sacrifice has saved us. Saved New Hope. Saved everyone."

He stood, and Tevy stood with him, then slumped into Kaiden's arms. "She has to live. She just has to. She's the only family I have left."

"I understand what you're saying, Tevy, and I pray with you. But she's not your only family." Kaiden hugged him tight. "You have a whole village that counts you as family. And you have the wolves." He set Tevy back, placing a hand on the boy's shoulder. "We're not going to let her die, all right? You and I and a lot of people back home will use every ounce of magic we have to bring her back from whatever chasm she's fallen into."

Tevy's eyes were bright with tears. He tried to suck them back. Kaiden knew his own eyes held unshed worry. He turned away, staring out at the winterscape beyond the cave. He knew if he didn't do something soon, he'd melt into a puddle of his own tears.

"We need to get her back to New Hope," Roulf said, coming up beside him.

"Agreed. Maybe Raisa can reach her. Her ability to help others heal is stronger than anyone else I know." He let out a long breath of air, trying to rid himself of the paralyzing fear that coursed through him. "I'll start cutting limbs for sleds."

"I'll go with you and look for brush. Tevy, stay with your sister."

Tevy nodded as Kaiden and Roulf headed out. They searched for anything that would help them. While they walked the area, Roulf brought up a name Kaiden had hoped never to hear again.

Taegar.

"That wraith is dead. Rianthe gave everything she had to kill her."

"That's the thing," Roulf said. "I'm not so sure she's dead."

Kaiden stopped slicing at wood and whirled on Roulf, knife still in hand. "What do you mean?

"I wish I didn't have to say this, but I doubt very much that Taegar was destroyed."

An anger that would not be tamped down flared in Kaiden and he whacked at the wood. "What makes you think she's not gone?" he finally asked.

"I spent some time searching the spot where she stood. There's nothing there. No body, no ash, no runes, nothing. You are aware of the druid way?"

"Return to the soil, ashes to ashes, right?"

"Yes." Roulf sat down with some wilted fronds and began weaving them together. "I believe she used her magic to...disappear. To somehow transport herself elsewhere. I wasn't even certain that was possible, but we have to consider it."

Kaiden tightened his lips for a moment, trying hard to get a grip on his anger. "As long as she's gone we are safe, at least for the moment. We have to get Rianthe home. And Hark. The rest—" Kaiden waved toward where Taegar had been. "That will have to wait."

"That's all we can do. Do not convince yourself that we are done with the Dark druid, though. More is to come. I'm certain of it."

Roulf stopped working and gazed at the cave, deeply frowning.

Maybe they weren't done with the Dark druid and maybe they were. Right now, Kaiden would focus on getting Rianthe home. He continued to slash at the wood, cutting pieces to form the shell of a sled, remembering the nights in Casper when he'd been so injured he had to just lie there while she worked. Rianthe had built a sled to carry him. He'd hated every helpless moment on it, had felt every bump and log.

It might be better if she remained unconscious until they got her home. She would not like laying on a sled any more than he did.

All his energy, beyond that needed to build the sled, went to hoping for the opportunity to tell her she'd slept through her bumpy ride. And to tell her other things.

~~~

Dinner came and passed by the time they completed the sleds. They decided to wait until morning to leave. It gnawed at Kaiden's gut to delay taking Rianthe back to New Hope but the weather had turned frigid over the course of the afternoon. A cold reminder that winter had not yet given way to spring. Traveling at night was too dangerous.

Kaiden settled in beside Rianthe, curling her into his arms. He would keep her warm and safe. That was the only way to help. He reached for her hand and tucked it beneath his on his chest. No reaction. Nothing. She was as limp as the noodles Kathra made. She might not come out of her deep coma and that petrified him. He kissed her hair. "Come back to me, Ri. You've got to come back. I can't live without you."

Through much of the night, he whispered to her about everything they would do when all this was over. How free they would be to enjoy life and each other. At some point, exhaustion took over and he drifted off, waking with a start as dark began to fade into day.

Morning dawned overcast, but no additional snow had fallen. Kaiden carried Hark, then Rianthe out of Origin cave and settled them on the sleds. He wrapped Rianthe's cloak tightly around her. The cold would be an issue. Precious time was spent finding her boots, along with more brush to put underneath and over them to keep them warm. Hardwood cocooned coals from their fire were snuggled next to each of them for additional warmth.

Finally, they were ready. Kaiden had fashioned some crude straps and now placed those around the wolves. He picked up his own strap. Roulf stood in front of Origin
~~~

cave, his head bowed.

"We're ready to go."

Roulf held up a hand for silence. The entrance shimmered, and what looked like rock materialized in its place. Roulf raised his head and drew a deep breath, as if trying to replenish his energy. "I safeguarded the cave. It's only an illusion, but hopefully, it will keep others from finding it until we can protect it properly. There is still magic here."

With that accomplished, the somber group bent their heads to acknowledge what they'd lost there, then began the long journey home.

CHAPTER TEN

Jonah stood at the edge of the Remembrance fields, gazing out through the trees. Impatiently waiting. Too many days had passed without word. He should not have allowed them to go. Worse, he'd actually endorsed the plan.

He'd sent the world's best hope off on a fool's errand. These were his children. New Hope's children. They'd gone off unprepared to the greatest battle of their lives and he had let them.

Kaiden, his son. True-named protector. Kaiden's power was strong, but with everyone's magic stifled by something they didn't understand, it wasn't strong enough.

Tevy and his wolves were all so young. Too young for this journey.

In the short time since Roulf had joined their village, Jonah had come to know him as a man of intelligence.

He'd been a good mentor, but was it enough?

Their best weapon, Rianthe, had not found the bulk of her magic, yet he'd sent them to take on the Dark druid.

Jonah bowed his head, worry weighing him down like a tree under heavy snow.

They'd been gone long enough to make it there and back twice. Why weren't they home yet? Had they perished? He'd expected some sign from Earth over the outcome of the battle. Lightning in the sky, or...a look of death. There'd been no word, no sign, nothing.

Jonah hit the tree next to him. A mound of snow dropped like dead weight on his head and shoulders.

He didn't care, but stood resolute, searching the woods for any sign of Kaiden and the rest.

Where were they? Bleak eyes searched through the trees. Why had he let them go? He should have gone with them.

"You couldn't have helped them." Raisa joined him, putting her arm around his waist.

Jonah settled his arm around her shoulder, hugging her tight, seeking the comfort only she could give. "You know me well, wife."

"I also know it wasn't your call to make, and even if you had gone with them, you couldn't have helped. Besides, you're needed here. They were as aware of that as you are."

"What you say is true, but it's hard not to second-guess. They should be home by now."

"They'll arrive in their own time. Yet..." She joined her husband in his search of the woods.

"What?"

"I don't normally have an extra sense. A few days

ago, at midday, something came over me. An...unshakable darkness.”

“You didn’t tell me.”

Her smile was timid. “I didn’t want to increase your worry.”

Jonah kissed Raisa’s forehead. “Please, let me know when you sense these things. I don’t want you worrying overmuch, either.”

Raisa’s smile widened, just for a moment. Jonah loved her smile. Her eyes, always bright, crinkled at the edges when she was happy, showing the lines of their years together. It was a map of their life and he loved it, and her.

Her smile dimmed as she searched the trees again. “Something happened. I know that, but I don’t think anyone died that day.”

He started to question her, but she held up her hand to silence him.

“I don’t know any more. It’s just...a sense I get.”

Jonah took a deep breath. “Then we’ll have to wait.”

Raisa stiffened beneath his arm. “Maybe we won’t have to wait so long.”

Jonah followed her gaze. There, in the distance, movement. Could it be? “Stay here,” he told her before he plowed through the snow.

It didn’t take long to meet the disheartened, bedraggled group that trudged home. There was no need to ask questions. Defeat clouded their eyes.

He hugged Kaiden, close and hard and long. “I’m so happy you’re safe, son.”

“Yes. *I’m* safe.”

“But not all of you,” Jonah said, stepping back.

“No,” Roulf answered. “Not all of us.”

Jonah saw past them now. To the two litters, pulled by wolves, weighted down by bodies. His breath caught in his throat. Rianthe? Tevy?

Jonah searched the wolves, found the telltale light color of Tevy's wolf, and let out a breath. Tevy was all right. But Rianthe?

"Rianthe and Hark were injured," Roulf said.

"And we need to get them home," Kaiden said, giving the signal to pull. Jonah reached for the strap Roulf had been using.

Raisa was not beside the tree where he'd left her. She'd gone to tell the village they'd returned and to prepare, he was certain. She knew some were injured without being told.

Most of the village stood waiting in the round when they arrived. "Come," Raisa said, beckoning to Kaiden. "We have beds ready in the keep."

Kaiden and Jonah picked up Rianthe and Hark to carry them inside and laying them on soft beds. Raisa had her herbs and medicines set out on a table nearby.

Kaiden smoothed back Rianthe's hair as he settled her. Jonah saw the lines of worry in his face. He gripped his son's shoulder. "She's home now. You've done what you can."

"Yes, you have," Raisa said. "You've done what you can. Now you need to take care of yourself and let me care for our beloved Rianthe."

"I'm not leaving her."

Raisa glanced at Jonah and his grip on Kaiden's shoulder tightened. "Yes, you are, son. You need to give Raisa time to do what she does best – assist in the healing. For both of them." Jonah gently led Kaiden out of the keep, nudging his reluctant feet forward.

"I need to stay with her," Kaiden said. "She needs to know I'm there."

"I get that." Jonah steered Kaiden toward the dining hut. "You won't be any good to her if you don't take care of yourself. Let's get something to eat. Then, get you cleaned up. By then, Raisa will have her patients settled and you can be with Rianthe."

The urge to return to her side was strong. Jonah saw it in Kaiden's face as he glanced back over his shoulder. Jonah looked back, too. Tevy, in wolf form, settled on the ground outside the doorway to the druid's keep. The other wolves joined him.

"See? The wolves will keep an eye on her. Come. Get something to eat and tell me what transpired. Raisa will tell you immediately if there's any change in Rianthe."

Once they were seated in the dining hut, Jonah encouraged Kaiden to take bites of the food Kathra set in front of him. While he ate, Jonah coaxed the story out of him about what had transpired at Origin cave. At some point during Kaiden's telling, Roulf joined them, digging into his own plate of food. He added bits and pieces to Kaiden's words.

Jonah grew more and more troubled as the story unfolded. "This is dire information indeed," he said when they'd finished. Things were worse than he thought. Would nothing ever change? Now, in the dead of winter, they were half-starved because the plants wouldn't grow, no matter how much little Ujami tried. He was just over five months old, and they dare not push the babe too far. He must grow and thrive himself before helping his home.

Game was scarce. Breakfast consisted of a thin

gruel-like concoction no flavoring would enhance, although Kathra worked her magic with seasonings on anything that would provide energy for their bodies. Dinner was rarely anything other than stew, with only enough meat to add flavor.

Thankfully, they'd managed to set aside a good amount of flour and yeast for the winter. They had bread. But bread did not sustain a body for long.

Now, their only hope for the future lay near death. Kaiden glanced out the door. Jonah followed his gaze, sensing the entire town's heart focused on Rianthe.

"You really think Taegar survived Rianthe's attack?" Jonah asked Roulf, turning back to the table.

"I'm almost certain of it."

"We've seen no change that would indicate an easing of our difficulties, so whatever was accomplished, it has not yet released Earth's *awen*," Jonah said. "The healing has not yet begun."

"Agreed. Our position is not good," Roulf answered.

Kaiden stopped eating to stare again at the tower where Rianthe lay.

Jonah tapped his elbow. "Eat."

He took one bite, then set his fork down.

Their troubles had no end in sight. Things were indeed dire. What options did they have? None. Yet it wasn't in Jonah's blood to do nothing. It hadn't been in Bhren's, either. He'd always known what needed to be done and which direction New Hope should choose. He'd brought them all there for that purpose. Without Bhren, Jonah struggled to find that vision and to determine what steps to take. Right now, he found it difficult to even think. So many bad things had happened. To his home, his friends. He looked at Kaiden. To his family. How would they get past this?

Nothing had ever come from morose contemplation, and that wasn't Jonah's style. He straightened, trying to shrug off the melancholy. "Well, to wallow in dark thoughts won't help us determine the next step. The entire focus of New Hope, and any magic we have, must be on helping Rianthe find her way back to us."

Roulf nodded and Kaiden, for the first time since they'd arrived home, looked hopeful.

With his hands on the table, Jonah pushed himself to stand. "Kaiden, let's get you to the showers."

"I'm going back to the keep," Kaiden said, standing.

"No. Go clean up first. Don't argue with me. You smell like a pig pen."

It lightened Jonah's heart to see the hint of a smile touch Kaiden's face.

"Once you're clean, and only then," Jonah wagged a finger at his son, "do you go back to the keep to sit with Rianthe and Hark. I agree that your time is best spent by Rianthe's side." Jonah clapped Kaiden on the shoulder. "Talk to her, keep her focused on coming back to us. You and Tevy can take turns. But I expect you to sleep, too. We'll set up shifts for the rest of the village to come and spend time with Rianthe, lending her their strength while focusing on her recovery."

"That sounds like a good plan." Kaiden's voice shook with emotion.

"And tell Tevy and those wolves to go for a swim. They smell as bad as you do."

Kaiden actually chuckled as Jonah pushed him toward the bathing house.

"He's got a powerful worry," Roulf said, standing beside Jonah.

"Don't we all?" Jonah sniffed, glancing at the little man beside him.

"I know, I know," Roulf said with a chuckle of his own. "To the bathing house with me, as well."

Jonah chuckled with him. It felt good. "Between the dank cave and pulling those litters for a few days, you all need it."

"Maybe, once we're all clean and get some sleep, we can help you figure out what's next."

"That would be good." Jonah turned serious. "Because I have absolutely no clue."

CHAPTER ELEVEN

"Do you think she'll ever wake up?"

Tevy. That was Tevy speaking, but Rianthe couldn't see him. Everything was dark. Pitch black. She tried to open her eyes, but they wouldn't budge.

"I don't know."

Kaiden. Rianthe cried out for him, but he didn't answer her.

She didn't deserve to be heard. Remorse weighed her down as effectively as death. She'd failed. Deep in her soul, Rianthe knew Taegar still lived.

For a short while, Rianthe had come to believe what Bhren, and even her father, had told her. What everyone else thought to be true. That she was the prophesied one. But that momentary faith had been her downfall, and she deserved whatever hell this was. Stuck in limbo, knowing how it would all end. Helpless to do anything but watch it unfold.

Taegar had won and Rianthe wanted to die. She'd let everyone down. Her parents, Bhren, Uja, Tevy. And Kaiden. She'd really let him down. He deserved so much better than she'd given him. Maybe this was how it should be. She would die and he would move on to someone stronger, more like him. Someone who would be his partner and help him fight Taegar or whatever else came their way.

Not her. She'd been weak. And now, she was dying.

Something soft encircled her hand. No. Someone. Tevy? It wasn't Tevy. It was Kaiden now. Her heart ached. *Please. Please just let me go. I don't deserve you. I don't deserve any of you.*

Let me die.

Please.

~~~

Taegar stared at the light pouring from Origin cave's altar. It had weakened much in the short time she'd been there. This was Origin cave, the place she'd known of since the magic had first appeared. Elusive. Damian Royan had hidden it well. But now she'd found it, along with the second stream of magic. Now, it was hers. Did that little girl and her foolish friends actually think they could drive out the most powerful druid ever to live?

She had only one place left to find. Then, with the talisman, she would finally release the magic and bind the strands together, making them subject to her whim for all time.

That must happen very soon. If the light here dimmed to the point of darkness, there would be nothing left. The magic would disappear forever and she would die.

To find the missing runes was essential to her plan
~~~

and time was running out. Taegar stewed. She was certain they'd been with the girl at some point. Rianthe Royan. Her enemy's progeny. She would pay dearly for her part in this delay. Her death would be slow and painful.

The runes had not been with the girl, but she'd reacted like an overprotective mamma bear when the brother's name had been mentioned. Tevy. He had Royan magic, too. Taegar had sensed him there, in wolf form. Most likely, he guarded the runes, then returned them to Damian's daughter who would protect them with her life if need be.

Fine. If the Royans wanted to protect those runes so badly, they would learn the consequences of their actions. Taegar thrust her hands into Origin cave's light and collided with Earth's resistance. She fought for what was hers until the *awen* capitulated and the energy flared and flowed directly into her.

She drank in the magic until she had enough for her plan. At the entrance of the cave, she looked at all the trees covered in white, the ugly, pristine snow that had not been disturbed since the Royan protectors had left days ago.

Their world was about to change. They would realize the ramifications of not bending to her will. Taegar held out her hands and magic flowed outward. Trees shriveled and turned black beneath their white blanket. Snow fell in earnest.

Still, the magic poured out of her, sending death in waves through the world. Earth shook, battling her even in its weakened state.

She would win.

She always did.

~~~

There had not been an earthquake in months. This one hit out of nowhere. Kaiden threw himself over Rianthe's still form as the tower shook around them. Dust and small rocks rained down on them. Taschia, who'd barely left Rianthe's side, whimpered. Hark, whose injuries had healed quickly, wasn't in the keep. He'd chosen to sleep with his brothers in the barn.

People screamed, reacting to the shaking. It lasted longer than any Kaiden had been through before. The ground shook and spasmed, accompanied by a loud rumbling. Then, after one big burp, calm replaced chaos. Calm and quiet. Deathly quiet.

Kaiden sat up, checking Rianthe to make certain nothing had hit her and there was no change in her condition.

She is no different than she was, Taschia mind-spoke to him. *Something else has changed.*

"What?"

I cannot see. Things are worse. That is all I know.

"Stay with her," Kaiden told Taschia. "I need to check on the rest of the village."

I will stay. Hark and my brothers come to join me.

"Are they all right?"

They are well.

Kaiden nodded, already out the door. Outside, people gathered in the round. Most of them looked dazed. A few were bleeding from minor scrapes. Fraka and Ujami came from the growing house and Kaiden rushed to their side.

"We're all right," Fraka said. "We huddled under a table. This time, we built the growing house extra strong. It held." Pride sat right beside the worry in her voice.
~~~

"Look!" Anniah, pointed as she clung to her husband, Mokie.

Everyone looked in the direction indicated and a collective gasp rolled through the crowd.

What Kaiden saw congealed like a bad piece of fish in his stomach. Evergreen trees laden with snow were shedding their needles. Branches drooped and snow plopped to the ground, so much that it sounded like an avalanche. The trees withered before their eyes, led by the stench of decay. In a matter of moments, the snow had given way to black, gnarled sticks where trees, cloaked in white, had stood proudly only moments before. The wave of death rolled over them. Even Kaiden gasped. No tree was left healthy. No shrub or fern survived the onslaught. Whatever sickness or disease had attacked their woods, it was complete.

The wave rolled around and through New Hope and continued on, like a death ripple spreading out. As one, the people of New Hope watched until the destruction rolled past them. Even then, they stared, some with hands over their heads, ducking. Others with mouths agape. A few had fallen to their knees, disbelief and despair written in the haggard lines of their faces.

Ujami started to cry and all eyes turned to Fraka, who tried to console him with little success.

"What happened?" she asked over the five-month-old's wail.

Everyone crowded around Kaiden, all asking the same question as Fraka. And Kaiden had no answer to give them. Everything was gone. Destroyed. Was this Earth's final message? That plants and trees were now unsustainable? If that were true, they were truly doomed.

Kaiden held up a shaking hand, trying to quiet

everyone, though he had no idea what to say to them. Each person looked at him, the hope fading from their eyes, the hope that had deserted them with each tree's demise.

Jonah rushed in from the now barren woods, panicked. Kaiden had never seen him panicked in all the years he'd known him. "I can't find Raisa."

"Where was she last?" Not knowing jolted Kaiden's heart. He couldn't lose her, too.

"She went to the growing fields to find more herbs to treat Rianthe." Jonah darted his eyes around like a wild man, not focused on anything, searching everywhere. "I've got to find her."

Kaiden tried to ground his father with a hand to his shoulder. "We will, father."

Gratitude eased into Jonah's crazed eyes as he nodded.

After he barked orders to the others to check on everyone and gather the injured, Kaiden motioned to Mokie and Tevy, who'd just joined them. "We need a search party. Raisa's—" Dram. His own voice broke. Would the bad news never end? "Raisa is missing. She was last seen heading for the growing fields. Let's spread out in that direction and search." He kept his hand on Jonah's shoulder. "You and I will search together. Fraka?"

Ujami's cries had simmered to air-gulping sobs.

"Can you stay with Rianthe until we find Raisa?"

Fraka nodded, disappearing into the keep with the babe in her arms.

They fanned out along the pathways. Kaiden and Jonah took the most direct route, the one Raisa should have taken. They slogged through all the snow and needles and searched everywhere along the path, but reached the fields without finding any sign of her. Not even a footprint in the snow.

The others joined them, shaking their heads. "Nothing," Tevy said, glancing at Jonah. "So far."

"Where is she?" Jonah asked, almost to himself.

"The herbs she grows are in the far section of the field." Kaiden led the worried group to that area.

"Footprints," Jonah cried. "She must have come the back way."

"The prints head off this way," Kaiden said, moving down the trail. Jonah and the others were close behind him.

"Help!" The voice seemed far off.

"Raisa!" Jonah cried. He passed Kaiden at a full run.

They found her, pinned and freezing, beneath a log. Jonah rushed to her side.

"I-I'm s-sorry," she said, her teeth chattering. "I needed more h-herbs, so I went l-looking—"

"Shh, shh," he said. "Save your energy." Jonah's smile was all for Raisa. "Are you hurt?"

"I th-think my arm is broken. I can't tell about the rest. I'm numb. I'm so c-cold." Her lower lip had started to tremble.

Kaiden assessed the situation. The tree had fallen dead straight across his mother's legs, but it looked like the limbs of the tree had prevented it from crushing her. He couldn't tell for certain and her numbness worried him. Leaning down, he smiled and patted her shoulder, exuding a calm he did not feel inside. "Try to stay calm, mother. We're going to get this monster off you."

Tears welled in Raisa's eyes and slipped out. Jonah wiped them away with a concerned glance at Kaiden.

She'd grown so pale.

Things looked grim. Kaiden yanked at a limb, tearing it from the tree like it was a toothpick. Branch after branch, he pulled the wood away so they had a clear area to work on the downed tree.

Mokie had run back to New Hope for help. Several men arrived.

"We need a small log and a long pole," Kaiden said. A fulcrum would be needed to lift this tree. They didn't need to move it much. Just enough to free his mother's legs and pull her out.

When most of the limbs were cleared, they rolled the short log in next to the tree, then set a pole to use as a pivot. All the men lined up, ready to put every bit of their strength into freeing the woman who'd doctored and loved them for so many years.

Kaiden knelt by his mother. He laid a calming hand on her shoulder. "We're going to lift the tree now. It might hurt."

Raisa nodded, her eyes wide. "I'll be fine, son. You be careful. All of you." Ever the nurturer. Kaiden gave her shoulder a comforting squeeze.

He glanced at Jonah, seeing his own concern reflected back. "One we relieve the weight, you and Mokie pull her out.

Jonah nodded.

With nothing more to say, Kaiden took his place at the end of the lever pole, his eyes stinging with tears.

"Ready?" he asked the men who'd positioned themselves at the pole.

"Ready," they said in unison.

As one unit, they pushed down on the pole. Kaiden poured all his strength into the effort. His face grew warm and his arms bulged as he pushed, praying all the while that the pole would not break.

At first, the tree didn't budge. The woods were silent except for the grunts of the men. Then, the long pole they were using made cracking noises.

Please, he begged. *Hold until we get her out.*

After what seemed like an eternity, Kaiden heard one creak, then another. "Keep pushing," he urged them. "Keep pushing."

"It moved," Mokie hollered. "Not enough, but it's moving!"

Kaiden renewed his efforts, and his friends did the same, pushing with every ounce of strength they had. Kaiden dug deep, the familiar warmth welling up in him. A warmth he only felt when in contact with – *Rianthe*? How could that be? He almost lost his grip on the pole. Had she awakened? Was she helping from her bed in the druid's tower, sending him strength?

There was no time to think it through. The power welled up in him and he used it, pushed harder, until the pole lay on the ground. They couldn't move it any farther.

"We've got her," Jonah yelled. "We're clear. Let it go!"

The men let go and leaped back, the tree crashing back to the ground. Kaiden barely noticed. He rushed to his mother, still thrumming with magic and strength and adrenaline that he couldn't quite tame.

Dirt flew as he skidded to a stop.

"How is she?"

"She's all right, I think," Jonah answered, cradling her to his body.

Kaiden's chest heaved. He searched for something,

anything to do. He needed action. Needed to rip something apart. He looked around the death-encrusted woods, searching for something on which to vent his fury.

Raisa laid her hand along Kaiden's cheek, pulling his attention back to her. "Rest, son. It's all right. I have no injury beyond scratches, bruises, and this arm."

He listened to her words through a fog. The wild magic still had him tight in its clutches.

"You saved me," she said. "Let the *awen* go. I'm safe. There's nothing more you need to do."

He didn't know how to let loose of the magic. This had never happened to him before, not to this degree. He needed an outlet, a way to pound it out.

Be still. Let it...flow out...naturally.

The words in his head, were they Raisa's? He looked at his mother, who stared back with concern.

The wolves?

It is not I who speaks to you, Taschia said.

Then who?

The words have her flavor.

Is she awake? Are you with her?

I am with her. No, she does not move or wake.

Then how?

Kaiden sensed what amounted to a mental shrug from the wolf.

Another puzzle. Kaiden tried to follow the suggestion from the mysterious mind-speaker. He closed his eyes and breathed deeply, willing the power to ebb. It dissipated slowly as he focused on letting go.

"Son." Jonah's summons got his attention. "We have to get Raisa back home."

Kaiden shook the confusion from his mind. The

wildness had receded. Not completely, but enough. "Can you tolerate being carried?" he asked Raisa.

She nodded. "Just be mindful of the arm."

He picked her up, but before they'd started out for New Hope, Raisa's cry of horror stopped them all. "What happened?"

They looked around, taking in the devastation.

"Some disease?" Tevy asked.

"This is no disease," Raisa said quietly.

"This is dark magic," Jonah finished. "And it does not bode well for us." He stared at the withered world around them, then turned to Kaiden. "First, we attend to Raisa. Then, we can discuss...this. Whatever it is."

Kaiden nodded and headed back to the village, carrying his mother gently. He walked straight to the hut she and Jonah shared and laid her down on her bed. "You have helped each person in this village find healing. How, now, can we help you?"

Raisa examined her arm, grimacing in pain when she tried to turn her wrist. With a whimper, she slowly tested the fingers of her hand.

"Stop," Jonah said, kneeling beside her bed. "You're hurting yourself."

"I must determine if the bone needs setting." She continued in silence, though the price of movement was evident on her face. Finally, she collapsed back onto her pillow.

"You're as white as a lamb in spring," Jonah said.

"That was not...easy," she answered. "But I don't think the bone needs shifting. I need small boards from the supply hut. Two of them. About as long as my arm from finger to elbow. And bandages to wrap them around my arm. Plus a sling to hold my arm. I must keep it immobile until it heals.”

"I'll get the supplies," Kaiden said. Jonah stayed by Raisa's side. He would make certain she bore no other injuries.

When Kaiden returned, he and Jonah managed to wrap his mother's arm with only a little additional pain.

"I didn't find any other major injuries," Jonah said.

"I'm so glad," Kaiden answered, squeezing his mother's uninjured hand.

"Me, too." Raisa's smile was short-lived. Once she directed them how to settle her arm on a pillow to keep it above her heart, she sank back into the bed. "I need to rest now."

Jonah looked at Kaiden. "I'll stay with Raisa. We'll talk later about what happened to the trees."

Kaiden understood. His father would not be able to concentrate until he reassured himself that Raisa would be all right. He pulled a chair close to his wife's bed and lifted her limp hand, cocooning it in both of his. Kaiden did the exact same thing when he sat with Rianthe. The thought made him grin, his first genuine smile in some time. It felt good to smile at this gesture, something he had in common with the father who'd raised him. The only family he'd ever had and the only one he ever needed. He'd grown up knowing he'd been sold to Jonah as a newling for nothing more than a bite or two of food. Now, after finding out he'd been loved by his first parents, who couldn't provide for him, Kaiden rebuked himself for all those years he'd wasted wondering why he'd been tossed aside. He had everything he needed in a family right there.

He left Jonah with the sleeping Raisa. Walking through New Hope, he realized just how tired he was.

Unnaturally so. Is this what happened to Rianthe when she used magic?

Rianthe. Kaiden rushed to the keep. Inside, he found Tevy with Taschia, Fraka, and the sleeping Ujami. Tevy spoke to Rianthe, trying to bring her back. He looked up as Kaiden sat on the other side of his sister's bed. "Raisa is all right?"

"She will be," Kaiden said. He ran his hands over Rianthe's limp hair, twirling a strand around his finger. "I swore—"

"What?"

"This is going to sound strange, but it's like she was there with me, in the woods, bolstering my strength so I could save Raisa."

Tevy stared at Rianthe for a long time before he answered. "Maybe she was. I felt something during all that. I don't know. Like an awareness? It...disappeared, though. Slowly. After you all came back to the village.

"Do you think her—" Kaiden whispered, unable to finish the sentence at first because it terrified him. "That her essence is leaving her body?" he croaked out. "That she was helping us on her way to the beyond?"

Taschia whined, but Tevy shook his head. "No, Kaiden. Look at her. She breathes slow and long. There's no indication the breath is about to leave her."

Tevy, only half Kaiden's age, always knew how to relieve worry. "You're older than your years, Tevy."

"Only because Fraka told me that exact same thing a few minutes ago."

Kaiden reached over and shook arms with the twelve-year-old, then ran his hand over Ujami's head. "I thank you both."

Tevy dipped his head for a moment, acknowledging

the gratitude.

"You're welcome," Fraka said. "I think she's aware, even though we don't see it. So maybe she made an unconscious effort to help us. To help you save Raisa."

Had she? If that was the case, then they might be able to reach her, convince her to come back to them. Kaiden watched her, searching for any small nuance that would show an awakening. He clutched the edges of her bed, hoping. He needed her to come back to him like he needed air to breathe.

CHAPTER TWELVE

Tevy watched Kaiden focus on Rianthe. These two were soul-mates. He knew it. The wolves did, too. The wolves said they shared the Forever bond, though they didn't yet recognize it. Rianthe must come back to them or Kaiden would be lost.

"I'm going outside," he said, not certain if Kaiden even heard him.

All the wolves but Taschia were out hunting. At loose ends for a rare moment, Tevy wandered out of New Hope, past the dead or dying foliage, past the growing fields that showed a dark taint—like dried, congealed blood—on the snow. He didn't stop until he got to the Remembrance fields. He sank into the snow at his brother's stone, wiping the white powder away from it. "Uja, I don't know what to do. So much is happening." Sitting there, hugging the cold stone, he told his departed brother about the woes that had made their lives even worse.

"How are we going to get past this?" He looked around. "How can we even survive now that everything's been laid to waste? I don't know how this has happened, much less how to fix it."

Taegar.

Whether whispered by the wind or his own mind, it was the truth. She'd ruined everything. Had some vile curse from her caused this new blight? Tevy had the gift of foresight, a touch of Rianthe's ability to access the *ehwaz*, or vision plane. He couldn't see and didn't dream her dreams, but he sensed things. At the moment, that sight failed him. He saw nothing but bleakness. He didn't know what to do. If only he saw things in visions like his sister.

Tevy dug through the snow to place his hands on the earth like Ri. He stayed that way for so long, he lost feeling in his hands. Nothing happened. Nothing at all. He slapped the cold ground, then tucked his hands under his arms to warm them.

Rianthe was supposed to free Earth's magic. If she didn't wake, that task would fall on his shoulders as a Royan. He must find a way to heal Earth. How could he do that, though? His ability was shift-changing and a bit of prescience, not communing with Earth. He needed help. Bhren had come to Tevy shortly after the Forever breath left him to explain how to rebuild the druid's keep, giving Tevy exact directions. The old druid had never appeared since.

The answer must lay in those runes. Ri had asked him to keep them safe when they'd taken on Taegar. Now, back in New Hope, he'd lain them around her neck, hoping that the runes would help heal her. They were an incomplete set, though, and had changed nothing.

Tevy jumped up. That was it. He needed the rest of the runes. He must make the talisman whole. Then, if Rianthe never woke up, he would try to fulfill the prophecy. He would become *sowilo*, the sun who saved Earth's *awen*. He would connect with Earth and release the bound magic for all time to begin the healing process.

Almost running back to New Hope, Tevy stopped just short of the village round. No one would let him go to Origin cave by himself. They probably wouldn't let him go at all. But that's the last place he'd seen the runes. They had to be there. Taegar had been destroyed so there was little danger involved. He needed to find them.

My brothers, he called to his pack. *I need your help.*

They bayed as they returned from an unsuccessful hunt. He mind-spoke his plan to them and shift-changed to his wolf form just as they joined him.

Tevy glanced back at New Hope through his sharpened wolf eyes. So much devastation. When would this end? Whatever this blight was, it had given him no choice. He must return to Origin cave and find the runes.

With a little luck, he'd be back before they even knew he was gone.

~~~

No! Rianthe screamed, but no one heard her. *Don't let him go. Please, no. Tevy, stay here. Wait for me.*

She struggled to surface from a deep chasm. No amount of struggling would raise her up. Her eyes would not open. She could only sense what was happening and wait for the fates to decide. Wake or die.
~~~

CHAPTER THIRTEEN

Tevy had never seen so much devastation. Was this Earth's dying song? A stench filled his nostrils. The stench of death. Not only had every tree shriveled into petrified wood, the foliage that should stand tall through the snow had disappeared. As had any food. The wolves had found no game to sustain them on their journey. By the time they reached Origin cave, they were hungry, cold, and depressed.

Still in wolf form, Tevy sensed Roulf's magic hiding the entrance. He'd never tried to dispel anyone's magic before. Not sure what to do, he shifted back to his human self and ran his hands over the rock that should be the opening into Origin cave. Had he brought them to the wrong spot? Tevy shook his head. This had to be it. He placed both hands on the rock, then jumped back when it disappeared, showing the entrance he remembered.

That was easier than he thought. Roulf hadn't been

kidding when he said his illusion wasn't much. Smiling, and with a sense of accomplishment, he led the way into the large outer chamber. The light emanating from the altar had dimmed since the last time he'd been there. That confused him. With Taegar gone, he expected the light to grow and strengthen. Had that battle been a tipping point, sending Earth spiraling past the point of no return? Based on Earth's reaction, the idea was plausible. No. Tevy refused to believe that. To heal Earth, more needed to be done, and now, he was the one who must perform that healing.

I do not like this place, Hark mind-spoke. *I sense badness. Danger.*

Tevy did, too, but he refused to be deterred. *It's probably leftover from when we fought Taegar. We must search everywhere for the bag.* Tevy sent a mental picture to the wolves and they spread out. Hark, who was still recovering from his injury, moved more slowly than the rest as he continued to sniff the air.

Things are not as they seem.

Tevy nudged his muzzle. *I hate this place, too. The sooner we find the runes, the quicker we can leave.*

Hark's nod was reluctant, but he followed Grog down the tunnel where they'd defeated Taegar. Marin and Joek took the other one. Tevy searched the main chamber, sniffing the walls, searching for any hint of air that might denote a hidden alcove or hole. When he found an indentation, he stood on two paws, his others braced on the rock. The druid's keep back home had this same symbol. The mark could not have formed naturally. Excited, Tevy tugged at it with his teeth.

Nothing happened. Maybe he needed to be in human form.

Before Tevy shifted, a wail sounded, freezing him for too long as he sniffed the air. Something was wrong.

Another wail.

Grog!

Tevy rushed down the tunnel Hark and Grog had taken, his heart pounding in his chest as he raced toward the sound.

Wolf howls were close now. Had the other wolves joined Hark and Grog already? What trouble lay ahead?

Without taking time to reason, Tevy flew into the chamber where they'd killed Taegar, fangs bared. His pack needed his help.

Hark!

His alpha lay on the ground, unmoving. The other wolves stood around him, providing a wall of snapping, biting protection.

Rianthe stood in front, facing off against...Taegar!

Taegar is dead.

She did not die.

Tevy stared at Rianthe. How had she woken up and gotten here so fast? It didn't seem like Rianthe, at least, not the flesh and blood version he'd grown up with. She was translucent, as if she wasn't really there at all.

Taegar stood in front of her, golden eyes blazing. Again, also translucent. Had Tevy and his pack become unwilling participants in one of Rianthe's visions?

He saw Hark's motionless body. This was no dream or vision. This was real. And Tevy's alpha was down. Tevy growled, aimed his body at Taegar and prepared to avenge Hark.

No. You must not fight, Rianthe mind-spoke. *Go, brother. Go now. I cannot hold her for long.*

But I must...

There's no time. Please. Take Hark. Get out of here. Get as far away from Origin cave as you can. Then you can take time to think. To mourn your brother. Now you must run.

Hark lay so still.

He does not move, Grog said.

How can that be?

She did it. The wicked one.

Taegar?

Yes. We came here, then she appeared and threw fire at Hark. Grog nudged his brother, his tail between his legs and his ears flat. *The breath has left him.*

How was Taegar alive? Rianthe had killed her.

Go, brother. Rianthe glowed as the magic, directed at the Dark druid, poured out of her. *Please. Now. You are in danger.*

She was right. There was no time.

We cannot leave our brother, Marin, the next eldest, said.

No. They couldn't leave Hark here on the cold, rocky ground. He must return to the soil from which he came. It took precious moments, but Tevy shifted and together, they managed to half-carry, half-drag Hark's body back up the tunnel and out of the cave. Tevy got one last glimpse of Rianthe, a shield of white magic in front of her. Then, she was lost to his sight as they turned a corner.

Once outside, tears flowed down Tevy's face as he picked up Hark's broken body. The burden was heavy for Tevy the human, but he needed to do this. To get his alpha away from this cave, away from Taegar. To atone in some way for his part in bringing Hark here to his death. The wolves flanked him as they made their way slowly through the dead world. When they reached what used to be a clearing that was now a wasteland, Tevy set Hark down.

Each wolf sank to the ground next to their fallen comrade. Tevy changed back into a wolf and raised his head to the winds with theirs, joining his pack as they howled their grief. Then he fell silent, overwhelmed with sorrow and guilt. He should have listened to Hark's omen. The trip to Origin cave had been his idea. He'd forced his pack, his family, to run headlong into danger, bent on his own mission. With no thought for their safety. His stupidity had killed his brother. He should have listened.

Hark, Hark, Hark, he wailed. *This is all my fault.*

Marin got up and sat on his haunches next to Tevy. *Our brother chose. He died well.*

Hark died because of me.

He died doing what he loved to do. Marin leaned into Tevy. *His death is not on your heart.*

Tevy understood the wolf mentality which left little room for guilt, only for survival or a proud death. His human heart didn't quite grasp that though. Tevy lay there, next to Hark, one paw on the still form of his pack leader and friend.

His brother.

His fault.

You must let this go. Marin nudged him again and Tevy dropped his head, paying homage to their new pack, to Hark, and to their new alpha.

I will try. Deep inside, in the place Tevy kept private from everyone, he knew he would never get over this.

CHAPTER FOURTEEN

"Tevy!" The first word from Rianthe's mouth in days was a full-on scream. She sat up abruptly, causing Kaiden, who'd been about to nod off beside her, to leap up, sword drawn.

"What the—" He stopped mid-sentence as he whirled in a circle, seeing no threat. Heart pounding, he stared at Rianthe. She was awake. Thank the gods, she was awake!

"Ri," he cried, hugging her.

She threw Kaiden's arms off with more force than he'd thought her capable of. "Tevy!" she shouted again. She seemed to be in a trance. Her eyes were glassy and unfocused, yet she stared at the wall in front of her. "I have to save Tevy."

"He's right here, Ri." Kaiden tried to soothe her agitation with his voice. "He's with his wolves here in New Hope."

She shook her head. "He's at the cave."

"The cave?"

"Origin cave."

"Tevy? That can't be." Kaiden wanted to calm Rianthe, but he wouldn't leave her to search out her brother. Not while she was in this state.

Rianthe pushed out in front of her body, as if she were shoving something away. "You cannot have him," she said to the wall.

"Who are you talking to?" Kaiden was about as confused as he'd ever been as he stared back and forth between the blank wall and Rianthe.

Her arms began to glow, then white light spread out in front of her like a translucent shield.

"You will not get past me. You will not harm him," she said, again talking to the wall. Sweat formed on her brow. Whatever she was in the midst of took a lot of energy. Kaiden put a hand on her shoulder to help, to give her some of his energy, but she shrugged it off. He got a quick glimpse of Origin cave. Just like Rianthe had said. And of Taegar, floating in front of her, aflame with golden light directed at – Rianthe!

"Go, brother. Go now. I cannot hold her for long."

Brother? Was she in the *ehwaz* plane? She wouldn't let him touch her, wouldn't let him help. Kaiden could only stand by and wait for this to play out. It was killing him.

"He is gone," Rianthe said.

Kaiden's heart stuck in his throat as her words froze him. *Tevy? Gone?*

"You cannot harm him."

Now, he caught the note of triumph in her voice. Kaiden let out the breath he'd been holding.

Rianthe cocked her head, glaring with intense fury in front of her. "You have done great damage to my family. I will return. And you will pay."

She listened to some unknown again, then the white shield in front of her brightened, almost blinding him before it disappeared. Rianthe fell back onto her bed mat, drawing air into her lungs in deep, heaving breaths.

Kaiden sheathed his sword and knelt beside her, grabbing her hand. "Ri. You're awake." The rest, what had just happened, that would get sorted out later. Ri had come back to them! Kaiden wanted to shout it to the highest mountain.

"Tevy," Rianthe gasped out between breaths. "I had to save him."

"What do you mean? He's here, in New Hope."

"No." She almost shouted the word, then gulped. Her next words were much quieter, and enough to chill his soul.

"Tevy's not here. He just tried to take on Taegar."

"How can that be?"

Rianthe grabbed Kaiden's tunic, pulling him closer. "When did you last see him?"

"I don't know. A lot's been happening. And I've been here with you. A day? Two? I'm sure somebody's seen him." Kaiden glanced out the doorway.

"He left three days ago. With his wolf pack. He went to Origin cave to get the runes back."

"No." Kaiden had gotten his world back with Rianthe's return to consciousness, but now it disappeared once again. "He can't have." He saw Taschia sitting by the door. "What does Taschia say?"

My brother is not here. None of them are. Taschia's words came through to them both.

Rianthe struggled to sit up. Kaiden steadied her, his arms around her shoulders. Once again, she pushed him away.

"Please, go," she said, nodding to the door. "Prove that I'm right."

"I'm not leaving your side."

"I'm all right, Kaiden. Just weak. I promise I'll stay right here. You won't believe me until you check. Please. Go."

Although he was reluctant to leave her, the set of her face was a familiar sight. She would not back down until he checked. "All right. But you stay right here. No standing, nothing."

"I will."

"I mean it, Ri. No moving."

"Just go. We need to help Tevy and we can't until you believe me."

"Make sure she stays down," he said to Taschia.

I will try, the wolf mind-spoke.

Kaiden left. He spent precious moments looking in Tevy's favorite haunts. The partially rebuilt barn, the kitchen with Anniah. "Have you seen Tevy?"

"Not for a while," she said, frowning. "In fact, not for quite a while. Where is he?"

Without giving an answer, Kaiden turned on his heels. He checked in on Raisa, who was awake and sitting up, her arm in a sling. Jonah was at her side. "Have you seen Tevy?"

"Not for a couple days, I think," she said, her brows drawing together. "I can't remember when exactly. Where is he?"

Kaiden's shoulders fell under the weight of what he'd found to be true. "He's gone back to Origin cave."

"What?" Jonah jumped up from his seat beside Raisa.

"Rianthe is awake. It was the strangest thing, but I can't get into it now. She says Tevy is at Origin cave and needs our help."

Raisa stood up. "Take me to see Rianthe."

"Absolutely not. You need to rest and heal yourself," Jonah said.

"I'm going. You can help me or I can do it on my own."

Were all the women in New Hope born with a stubborn streak? Kaiden and Jonah helped Raisa stand. Kaiden tried to pick her up, but she swatted his arms away. "I broke my arm, not my legs. I can walk."

"You may not have broken your legs, but I've seen the bruises there and know you are not unscathed."

"You're right," Raisa said with a pat to Kaiden's cheek. "But I'm still going under my own power."

En route, Raisa asked Mokie to tell Anniah to bring water and food to the druid's keep. By the time they reached Rianthe, she was standing. Not well, but she was upright. Kaiden glared at Taschia, who sent him a mental shrug.

She has her own mind.

"Dram it, Ri. You said you'd stay down."

"You took too long."

Kaiden and Jonah exchanged glances, sharing their frustration. Rianthe wouldn't sit back down, so Kaiden stood beside her, letting her lean on him for balance. "You've been in a coma for days. You shouldn't be up so soon."

"I'm not the issue here. Tevy is. We have to get to him."

"You're not going anywhere."

"Then you have to go."

"I'm not leaving—"

She grabbed his tunic. "You *have* to."

Taschia, who'd stayed quiet by Rianthe's side, whined her agreement.

Jonah held up his hands. "Let's calm down so we can talk about this. Rianthe, you're about to fall over. Sit down." His voice brooked no disagreement. Surprisingly, Rianthe let Kaiden help her sit on her bed mat.

Jonah helped Raisa sit next to Rianthe. "We can't go anywhere without some information," he said. "What happened?"

Rianthe took a sip of the water Anniah handed her. "I was in a deep, dark place, buried in guilt. I—I thought I was dead. That this darkness was my punishment."

Kaiden reached for her hand and Rianthe held tight. She turned to him. "I heard you. You kept me from...disappearing completely, sinking into the muck of my pain-filled soul. When your voice drifted through, it gave me hope."

A mist clouded Kaiden's eyes, blurring his vision. All the days, talking until he was hoarse. It had worked. "I couldn't lose you, Ri. You're my world."

She nodded, her own eyes moist. "Then I sensed her."

"Taegar?" Jonah asked.

"She's dead," Kaiden said. "I saw it myself."

"Roulf doesn't think so," Jonah reminded him.

Rianthe shook her head. "Not dead. Disappeared. She shielded herself from all of you. You only thought she'd died. It would...it *will* take a lot more than what we did to end Taegar's plans." She shuddered and Kaiden pulled her into his chest, warming her with his own arms.

"From where I lay mired in nothing but my own stupid remorse, I was tossed into the *ehwaz*. I was in Origin cave. Taegar was there. So was Tevy, in wolf form. With his pack. He went to find the talisman." Tears spilled from her eyes. "He thought the cave would be empty and he planned to search for the runes. With me...gone, he thought my task had passed to him and he'd need the runes to save Earth and humanity. He didn't find them. Instead, he found Taegar." Rianthe squirmed out of Kaiden's arms, her voice rising again. "We have to get to him. We have to help him. She'll kill him. Or worse."

Kaiden moved with her, holding her until she stilled, using quiet words to calm her until they reasoned this out. "When you woke, you sat up, your arms straight out in front of you. A white wall of light appeared."

Rianthe nodded. "A shield made from my magic. I didn't know I was capable of that until I just...summoned it. It held Taegar back. She couldn't get to Tevy."

"You saved him." Raisa touched Rianthe's hand.

"I'm not certain. I yelled at the wolves to escape. One of them was down. I couldn't tell which one. I saw them dragging that wolf up the tunnel. But then Taegar attacked me with force. I held the shield as long as possible. When it dissipated, I lost the vision." She turned in Kaiden's arms, clutched them. "I don't know which wolf was injured. So you see? We have to go find them. We have to help, to make sure Tevy's all right."

"You're right," Jonah said. "We have to send someone to help."

By now, a small crowd had joined them, some inside, some listening from beyond the door.

"Kaiden," Rianthe said. "It has to be you. You're the

only one who can protect them."

"You need me."

"I'll stay," Jonah said, putting his arm around his wife. "We'll take care of Rianthe."

Raisa nodded. "We all will."

Murmurs of assent and nods validated her statement.

Jonah gestured to Mokie, who crouched down beside him. "Go with him, Mokie."

He nodded. "It would be my honor."

"Sam, Rhand, will you come, too?" asked Kaiden, turning to the crowd.

Both vehemently gave their consent. Kaiden didn't want to go. He didn't want to leave Rianthe, but the truth in her words hit home. It had to be him. Especially if... No. He refused to think about that. Tevy was alive. He had to be.

"All right," he said. "We leave within the hour."

The crowd backed out of the small room as Jonah helped Raisa up. "Time for you to rest."

Soon, it was just Kaiden and Rianthe. She hugged him tight. "Thank you."

"I would go anywhere to save Tevy. But you *must* take it easy and get your strength back," Kaiden said, cupping her cheeks so she'd look at him. "Promise me, Ri. I can't focus on Tevy and worry about you at the same time."

"I promise," she said without hesitation. "I really, truly promise. Please, get to Tevy."

He searched her face, saw her resolve, and recognized that for this once she would do as he asked. Kaiden's heart lifted for a moment. "I will, Ri. And I'll do everything in my power to bring him home safe."

"Come home safe. You're my world, too," she said.

Then, surprising him, she leaned in and kissed him. Sweetness, filled with promise. He could barely tear himself away.

CHAPTER FIFTEEN

Kaiden, Mokie, Rhand, and Sam caught up to Tevy and the rest of the wolves late the next day, having pushed themselves hard to get to them.

What they found about broke Kaiden's heart. A safe distance from Origin cave, the wolves surrounded the body of their alpha, Hark, amongst the gnarled, dead trees. Mourning and half-starved, they barely lifted their heads in greeting. Mokie, Sam, and Rhand all got food out of their packs for the wolves.

"I'm so sorry," Kaiden said as he sank to the ground beside Tevy. He set his hand on Tevy's wolf-head, scratching his ears.

Tevy never budged. He stared at Hark, head on paws. He grieved, a feeling all too familiar to Kaiden, one he would likely never forget. Too many bad things had happened in the past year. He surveyed the death all around them. When would it end?

"Here's food," Mokie said, handing him meat they'd brought with them.

Kaiden offered it to Tevy. Not even an ear twitched.

"You have to eat," he said.

No response. Had he lost Tevy, as well? To grief and despair?

"Come on, Tevy. Look at your brothers. They're eating."

Tevy lifted his head and looked around. *I'm glad they eat.*

Relief flooded Kaiden at the words in his mind. At least Tevy would talk to him. "They set a good example."

I'm not hungry.

"From what little I know, you haven't eaten in days."

It doesn't matter. Nothing matters anymore.

"It does to me. And to Rianthe. And all of New Hope."

Tevy's ears perked up. He stared at Kaiden, who saw the wolf tears matting his fur. He was in so much pain. Kaiden needed to pull Tevy back from this dangerous precipice.

"She's awake, Tevy. Your sister is awake. She'll be all right."

He saw a spark in Tevy's eyes, a fleeting sign of interest. Too soon, they dulled again, and he settled his head back down on his paws to gaze at Hark's body.

The other wolves devoured everything. If Kaiden didn't get Tevy to eat... No. He wouldn't go there. "You can't bring him back, Tevy."

It should be me, not Hark.

"How can you say that?"

This was my task. Not his. I shouldn't have brought him along. I shouldn't have brought any of them.

"Then you would be dead."

Yes. The plaintive sound of his voice scared Kaiden.

"Shift-change, Tevy. Please. Let's talk."

We talk now.

"I mean, man-to-man."

I honor my fallen brother in this form.

Since Tevy hadn't responded to friendship, the only step left was to force the issue. "You don't honor your sister."

Tevy lifted his head again and stared at Kaiden with the eyes of an aged wolf. Marin trotted over and nudged Tevy, but Kaiden was not privy to their communication. Whatever Marin said seemed to work. With the slowness and demeanor of an aged wolf, Tevy stood. First on four paws. Then, as he shifted, naked on two feet.

Kaiden pulled the clothes he'd brought for Tevy out of his pack and he dressed, shivering in the cold air.

"Happier now? Not even this honors my sister. I'm incapable."

"You're not incapable." Kaiden had won a small battle. He'd need to tread lightly to win the war. He needed to bring back the happy boy he'd known his whole life. To help Tevy find his smile again. Otherwise, the boy would be stranded in a dark place. "From what Rianthe told me, your pack exhibited great valor in this...situation."

"It wasn't enough. We couldn't save my brother. I couldn't." Tears streamed down Tevy's face as he crouched beside Hark, brushing a hand along his fur.

"Hark died saving his pack. Honorably."

"He shouldn't be dead at all! He's here because of me." Tevy screamed to the woods, the soil, the air. "It's all my fault!" Over and over, he screamed those words.

While his brother wolves watched him. Mokie, Sam, and Rhand kept their heads down, busy building a fire to melt snow for water.

Kaiden stood by and let Tevy scream. Let him get it all out. After a few minutes, he pulled the shaking boy into his arms. Tevy hit him. Again and again, sobbing the whole time, screaming the same words. "I killed him. It's my fault."

With a grief so powerful, it took a long time for Tevy to become exhausted. Even then, his sobs were heart-wrenching. Kaiden cried with him. They all did, wolf and man. Hark would be missed. He hadn't just been these wolves' pack alpha. He'd been an integral part of life in New Hope. His courage and determination to help all succeed would be sorely missed. As would his ability to keep young Tevy from attempting stunts beyond his abilities. Like the time Hark threw himself against Tevy when the pup tried to jump a ravine too big for him. Hark had almost fallen over the precipice himself. Kaiden and Rianthe had simply stood back and listened to the growls Hark sent Tevy's way for the next couple of days.

Hark had been family to all, and the hole left by his death would always be there. Kaiden held on to Tevy, trying to assuage his own grief as the boy cried.

Finally spent, Tevy sank into Kaiden's embrace. Kaiden sat down, taking Tevy with him, warming him against the emotions and the cold.

"I want you to understand," he said. "I've been where you are. In such a dark, guilt-ridden place I didn't think I'd ever come back from it. For a long time, I didn't want to. I had caused what happened. It was my fault. I needed to pay." He kept his voice low and quiet although it wasn't easy to rehash these memories.

Tevy lay still, his breaths ragged with spent emotion, but he listened.

"I didn't cause what happened back in Minor Town, where children—died," Kaiden continued. "That was all in place before I knew anything about it. It took me a while to realize I couldn't have stopped it no matter how hard I tried."

"But I—" Tevy's voice broke. "I asked him to come with me on a foolhardy mission. I shouldn't have p-put him in danger like that."

"You didn't know Taegar was still alive."

"I should have guessed. Something was off. I should have waited."

They sat there like that for a long while, going back and forth between silence and whispered words. Only Tevy could work through his grief. What Kaiden could do, though, was give him a ray of hope. "You're the reason Ri woke up, Tevy."

Tevy lifted his face to look at Kaiden. "I saw her. In the cave. I think—I think she saved us."

"She said you were in danger and she journeyed to the *ehwaz* to help you. She also said the pack fought valiantly and all she did was give you time to escape."

"No. She saved us, Kaiden. Hark—" He glanced at the still body. "If Rianthe hadn't been there, we might all be like him."

Kaiden hugged him. "This was not the outcome you wanted."

"We didn't get what I came for."

"The runes?"

"Yes," Tevy whispered.

"We'll find another way. You, Rianthe, New Hope. We all will. Together." Kaiden turned Tevy's face up so he would see the seriousness in his own. "No more running off on your own, all right?"

With another glance at the still form of his furred brother, Tevy nodded.

"Now, how about we get some food into that growling stomach of yours and set about preparing for the *kenaz*, to honor our brother Hark and give him back to the soil from which he came?"

With a heavy sigh, Tevy stood, taking the hardtack Kaiden held out, and the bread Sam handed him. He chewed slowly, still deep in thought, but at least he chewed.

It eased Kaiden's worry considerably.

"Does it ever get easier?" Tevy asked quietly as he ate.

The guilt. Kaiden understood and wouldn't lie to the boy. "It will always be with you. But perspective comes with time. The guilt settles in a corner of your heart and you become happy again. Mostly. And wiser."

"I wanted to die, like Hark."

"I know." Kaiden breathed a sigh of relief that Tevy had used the past tense in that statement. He wasn't over this, and might never be, but for now, he was turning back to the present, and the future. A good sign.

After Tevy had eaten, they built a pyre to honor Hark.

Tevy picked up the broken body of their brother. The burden was nearly too much for the boy, but Kaiden stood aside and let him proceed. He understood. This was part of Tevy's journey.

The wolves flanked him as he trudged to the pyre without a single misstep. He laid Hark's body on the wood.

"This isn't Hark anymore," Kaiden said to all. "This is only a shell. His spirit, his *hagalaz*, now soars through the skies and beyond. He died a warrior's death, giving his life to protect those he loved. An honorable death."

Hark. Friend. Brother. Alpha. He took care of us all, Marin, the pack's new alpha, said as Tevy repeated his words for the humans. *We honor you and send your body back to the soil from which you came. You will be forever missed.*

The wolf keens started, growing in intensity. Kaiden and the others joined in, grieving for their lost friend as Tevy set fire to the platform on which Hark's body lay.

So much death. All because of one evil druid's desire to live forever. It was unfathomable to Kaiden. He turned away, more tired than he ever remembered being. How would they recover from all this grief?

Tevy came up and hugged Kaiden, his tears not yet ready to dry. "I miss him already. So much."

Kaiden squeezed him tight, watching the fire burn, listening to the low keen of the wolves around them. Tevy joined in with his human voice, humming low, one last homage to Hark's sacrifice and his own grief.

"You'll miss him for a long time. We all will."

So much sadness permeated each of them, it was quite a while before they moved. How were they to bear it? Finally, when the fire had burned down to glowing embers, they said their final goodbyes to the brave wolf no one would ever forget. They began the journey home through a land destroyed by some virus that had struck with far too much speed to be caused by natural means.

"I can't believe everything that's happened," Mokie said to Kaiden as they walked. "Anniah and I were talking before we left. We don't have enough food stores to last long. Maybe another couple of weeks."

"We'll have to decide as a village what to do once we get home."

"Do you think we'll have to leave New Hope?"

With Anniah pregnant, Kaiden understood Mokie's worry. "I can't imagine this decay is local just to us. It hit too fast and spread wider and wider." Kaiden stopped there. He didn't want to put voice to his worry. This seemed like the last stand. Like Earth and mankind had just been handed a death sentence.

He saw no way out of the death that Taegar had rained upon them. It had to be Taegar. A burning anger grew within Kaiden and he picked up his pace, anxious to get back to New Hope.

To find a way to destroy that which was bent on destroying them.

UPRISING

CHAPTER SIXTEEN

Rianthe stayed true to her promise to Kaiden when he left to help her brother. She took it easy. Mostly. Laying around waiting had never been a strength of hers. Every time she closed her eyes to rest, worry overrode any attempts at relaxation. Worry for Tevy, for New Hope, for the survival of, well, everything. And everyone.

To keep the worry at bay, instead of resting she worked hard to regain her strength. She ate the rations given to her. She hated it. What little food remained should be given to others. Especially Anniah, who ate for two. This was too much like Kaiden's entry into this world. His parents had died from starvation trying to keep their newling alive. That couldn't happen here. She wouldn't allow it, which meant she needed power to fight. So she ate and regained her strength. First, she tested how it felt to sit up in her little room, and to stand.

Then she walked around and around the circle of her tower until she felt strong enough to step outside. She'd wanted to cry at what she saw there. Everything was dead or dying. The devastation was complete. Nothing lived, except the villagers. Neither rabbit nor rodent stirred, from what Anniah had told her.

Back in the tower, Taschia informed her that Kaiden, Tevy, and the others were on their way home. They were close enough now that Taschia could hear them. The news that Tevy was alive lifted a monumental weight off Rianthe's shoulders, but then her sister-wolf told her the rest. That Hark had given his life to protect his pack. Taschia slumped to the floor, keening her grief. Sarsa, an old wolf now, hobbled over and laid next to Taschia, howling for her lost son. All Rianthe could do was sit beside them, hugging them and smoothing their fur. *You are not alone. I grieve with you.*

There were no words to define their grief, so they sat there, head on paw and arm around furry body, for a long time. Remembering, saying goodbye, hurting. They would all sorely miss their friend, their son, and their brother.

So many terrible things had happened. In the space of a few full moons, everything had changed more than Rianthe thought possible. Before her True-Naming five years ago, her life had been uncomplicated. Yes, a cloud had hung over them of some forthcoming danger. Bhren had made certain they all remained aware of that. But it had seemed distant and difficult to realize as their true future.

Everything Bhren told them had become the horrible truth. In a short amount of time, they'd been beset by fire, death, and famine. Danger lurked around every turn, and

Rianthe saw no end in sight.

Rianthe, who had been prophesied to end their suffering, had no idea how to make that happen. Everything she'd tried so far had made things worse, not better. And now, Taegar seemed poised to win this war.

Laying with her head against Taschia, Rianthe drummed her fingers on her sleeping mat, restless, needing understanding. How bad were things? Only one way would lead to answers. She'd have to enter the *ehwaz*. The place of pain and battle. If she directed her thoughts, she might find out how far this death had spread. She huffed. So far, directing the visions had rarely been successful.

Before she could talk herself out of it, she pulled off her glove and walked to Bhren's old table, with its central repository of soil. The last time she'd dug her hands into the well of soil that filled a rock-tube from Earth's ground up to this table, she'd been devastated by her own True-Naming. None of that mattered now. Rianthe laid her hand on the dirt.

Earth. How fare you?

She kept her focus on Earth, picturing the trees of the Rushmore Woods, trying not to call forth the Dark druid.

Like a slow-moving mirage in the heat of summer, Earth appeared in front of her, zooming in until mountains separated from sky and trees from lakes. Treetops became blurry trunks as the vision raced through them, stopping in front of...

Origin cave! No! Rianthe tried to swerve the vision, to run. She could not tangle with Taegar again. Their recent battle had taken just about everything from her. Weakness held her back.

Her attempts to leave failed. She was held in place

by the vision.

A light blasted out of the cave. Rianthe ducked, certain the battle began anew. But the light didn't hit her. Rianthe followed it, saw it hit the trees above her. From the top down, they withered and browned. First one tree, then another. The ground around her turned dark, ferns and plants shriveled as the death moved from tree to tree.

The vision took her again. Up, up, up, high into the sky, where she saw the effect of this destruction. Green and blue alike turned foul and withered and dark. A rolling disease encompassed the area around Origin cave, then spread in all directions like an out-of-control ripple.

The wave of decay rolled over New Hope and beyond, growing larger and larger. Before long, Earth had nothing left to offer humanity. The devastation was total and complete. No food, no foliage remained. Only humans and a few animals, neither of which would last long without sustenance.

The vision released her with reluctance as Earth's dying tears stained her tunic. Such a deep sadness, tinged with a finality she didn't want to believe.

The end is near, the winds whispered. *I am almost gone.*

Rianthe raised her hand from the soil to see the tower once again. Taschia licked her tear-streaked face, but even that did not ease the pain in Rianthe's heavy heart, though she clutched her friend tight.

Rooted deep in her melancholy, Rianthe almost missed the commotion outside. Taschia's ears perked up for the first time since they'd heard about Hark, and she stood. Sarsa struggled to join her.

My brothers are home, Taschia mind-spoke.

She bounded out of the tower, needing to see them,

to know for herself that they were all right. Rianthe needed that, too. Yet, she stood slowly, still awash in the somber reality she'd just witnessed. Rianthe tried to shake it off and just be happy that Tevy was home. It wasn't easy.

Outside, everyone milled around the men and the wolves. And one twelve-year-old boy. Safe. The dark circles under his eyes, visible as Rianthe walked up to him, increased her worry. She stifled it and pulled him into her arms, hugging him like he was the lifeline that would get her, get them all, through this.

"Ah, Sis. Stop. I'm all right. Really," Tevy said.

"You scared the heck out of me, little brother." Rianthe set him back, looking him over again, searching for wounds she might have missed. There were none, save for the hidden ones only time would heal.

"I scared myself," he said with a very grown-up quiet.

Rianthe found Kaiden and mouthed her thanks. He dipped his head in acknowledgment, his sadness-tinged eyes bearing witness to the grave danger the wolves had survived. Except one. Roulf settled a heavy hand on Rianthe's shoulder, giving silent support for their shared grief.

Together, they walked into the dining house. Rianthe and Tevy and sat on a bench with the table behind them. Kaiden and the others sat across the table. Kathra handed Tevy and the men plates with meager fare on them. Most of New Hope had eaten already, but rationed food did not go far to assuage anyone's hunger.

Tevy picked at his food until finally, he pushed it toward Rianthe. "Give this to someone else. I'm not hungry and it shouldn't be wasted."

"You need to eat."

"I can't right now. Anyway, we ate most of Kaiden's rations on the trail. I'm fed."

Rianthe glanced at Kaiden, his nod affirming Tevy's statement.

While she'd prefer Tevy ate again, she'd have to be content he'd eaten recently, so Rianthe handed the plate off to Raisa, who'd sat down next to them.

"No. I've had dinner. Let someone else have it, someone who needs it more."

"Eat," Jonah said, sitting next to his wife. "You must heal yourself just like anyone else with injuries. You need the energy."

They were right to give Raisa the food. She looked tired.

She lowered her head for a moment, took a bite of food, then slid the plate to Anniah across the table. "You're eating for two, daughter. Let's share it."

Anniah looked around at all the faces. "I can't."

"You must," everyone said with one voice.

With grateful tears in her eyes, Anniah took a bite, then passed it to Fraka. "Feed Ujami the rest. He's our best food grower." Even though he was only a few full moons old, Ujami's ability was stronger than his father's. Uja had coaxed extra growth out of any plant, even before his True-Naming. Ujami only had to touch a plant and it turned green. Or had, until this recent devastation.

Rianthe couldn't stop touching Tevy. She was driving him nuts, but he'd just have to deal. She needed him to survive, to live. Yet, deep down inside, she accepted that none of them would live much longer if no food were found.

Most of the village had gathered with them and

worry deepened the furrows in every face. Kathra wrung her hands as she stepped closer. "Our food stores are very low. Almost non-existent," she reported. "Whatever blight killed the surrounding woods also got to the growing hut. Everything has been decimated."

Even the smallest among them reacted. Ujami whimpered and Fraka tightened her hold on him.

Mokie raised clenched fists until Anniah wrapped her arms around him. He pulled her in tight, kissing her long, dark hair with a tenderness that did not match the fear and anger in his eyes.

Some whimpered, others groaned. All understand the finality of what Kathra had told them.

"The destruction is complete. Nothing survived. I can't even find a viable seed."

Fraka spoke up. "We tried to rekindle the growth, but even Ujami was unsuccessful. Whatever happened, it's hampered his ability to bring the growth back. He's only six months old, so I won't push him to touch anything else until we have a better idea what's going on."

"There's no game, either," Jonah added. "With no food for them to eat, the animals have either perished or moved on to search for greener pastures."

"There are no greener pastures," Rianthe whispered.

"You've seen this?" Kaiden asked, reaching for her hand.

She nodded. "A vision. The taint is moving across all of Earth's lands. Very soon, nothing will be left."

Complete and total silence filled the room. Even Ujami, in Fraka's arms, grew quiet. All understood the truth. If a new way to grow food was not found, they would all die. And soon.

Rianthe glanced around. No one looked directly at

her. In fact, they appeared to be avoiding her, yet she felt the weight of their worry on her shoulders. She was supposed to fix this. She'd been designated to save them all. The solution must lie within her.

Once again, she had absolutely no idea what to do. She pulled her hand from Kaiden's and stood. "I'm sorry. I don't know how to fix this."

Kaiden stood beside her. He put his arm around her shoulders. "This isn't your fault." By turns, he met the gaze of everyone gathered there with them. "The answer will come when it's needed. We all must believe that or it won't happen."

"Agreed," Jonah said, taking a spot beside Rianthe and Kaiden. "Do not take this blame on your shoulders, Rianthe. You didn't create this. And whether you resolve it does not lay solely on your shoulders. We must all hope. All believe. All work to find a solution."

One by one, each person reached out to the next. When the last person connected, they became a village of one mind, a woven fabric of believers that filled Rianthe with an overflowing love. And, something more. An energy thrummed within them.

Humbled and overwhelmed by their belief in her, Rianthe bowed her head. "I need some time," she said. Slowly, they parted for her. Kaiden walked her out.

"Can you help me?" she asked.

He hadn't let go of her shoulder. He squeezed it now. "Always."

"I want to go to the lake. To our spot. To think."

She'd expected him to berate her and tell her it was too far for her to go. She wasn't strong enough yet. Instead, he lifted her in his arms without hesitation.

Rianthe had always been the strong one. Always led

the way, rarely asking for help. So this request hadn't been easy. Now, in his arms, she was very glad she had asked. For once, she didn't have to be the strong one. For this moment, she could just be here with Kaiden. The rest, she'd sort out when they reached the tree they'd often lain against.

This being carried thing? She wanted more.

Kaiden smiled down at her as he walked with an easy step. "Whatever your ladyship wants. I'm yours to command."

Yes. This was something she could definitely get used to.

CHAPTER SEVENTEEN

Kaiden set Rianthe on her feet with obvious reluctance. His arms stayed around her, offering both a steadiness she needed right now and a reminder of everything left that was good in this world. His eyes were dark green pools of emotion. Love, respect, fear. All mirrored by her own soul. This was where she wanted to be. Forever.

They climbed together, Kaiden following Rianthe's lead, to the outcropping of rocks that had been their spot since Rianthe first arrived in New Hope. Not that dratted druid's tower. She'd never know why Bhren had wanted it there, in that shape and that spot. She'd never liked it when she'd trained there and still didn't care for the place.

Here, she could think. Rianthe took a moment to catch her breath when she reached the top. That dark place she'd been mired in had wiped her out. Not moving for several days took its toll on the body.

Rianthe surveyed the area from her viewpoint. Things looked so different now. Shriveled and dying. Rianthe looked at the lake. The dark green color of winter had surrendered to an unusual silver tinge. She pointed. "Are those dead fish floating on the water?"

Kaiden scowled as he followed her gaze. "Sure looks that way, and probably tainted."

They both understood what that meant. Another food source annihilated, poisoned by Taegar's darkness.

Trees full of pine needles a few short days ago now stood gnarled and twisted, petrified by disease. Only the oak tree she and Kaiden sat under stood proud. Devoid of leaves, it stared this blight in the face and refused to surrender. Except new growth should be showing by now. Spring was upon them, yet nothing validated the passage from winter into a season meant for growth.

"This is bad," Kaiden said. "Everything's been affected."

Rianthe nodded. "In my vision, no place escaped this carnage. It kept spreading further and further. Earth is in its final throes."

How was she supposed to fix this? How could she be the person meant to heal...everything? At the first sign of real trouble, her body had gone into hiding. Yet now was not the time for questions. Now, she needed answers. A clear direction. A pall had overtaken Earth, and getting past it could not be a solitary endeavor. She needed help.

Shattered by darkness, the magic vanished.
It lies in wait for one who's banished.
Hidden power will blossom anew,
Only by passing the darkness through.

She'd been banished, first by her father when—trying to protect her—he told her to run, then by her own self. She'd also been through the darkness. Yet she saw no way to reach the light. Rianthe walked up to the venerable old oak. She pulled her gloves off.

"Ri," Kaiden said.

"I need answers."

"Everything's diseased. You don't know how it will affect you. And you've barely recovered from your own injuries."

"There's no other choice."

"I can't lose you."

Rianthe turned to Kaiden, whose wide eyes were filled with panic. She stepped toward him, into his open arms. Reaching up, she showed him her bare hands, cocking her head to ask his permission. He gave it without hesitation and she smiled her gratitude and her love. Nothing around them mattered in this moment. Only her, staring into his trusting green eyes as she cupped his cheeks.

The warmth came quickly this time. Her hands tingled with it, her arms conduits for the spark that was Kaiden's energy. A gentle green, like his eyes, that enveloped her in a cocoon of love and admiration.

Everything that was Kaiden flowed into her. His single-minded need to keep her safe, his love, and his heart, finally at rest about his past. He drew in a deep breath as if he wanted to take in all of her. She opened her mind and her heart and let him glimpse it all. All her fears, her insecurities, her devotion to him and to humankind. Her weaknesses and her strengths. She gave it all to him.

He lowered his lips and she wrapped her hands around his neck, keeping contact and urging him on. Their first touch, tentative and gentle, stripped everything unhappy away from Rianthe and filled her with unyielding love and a promise of a bright future together. His promise. He moved his lips over hers and she gladly reciprocated. There was no need for words. They heard them in each other's minds, sensed them in each other's hearts, and felt them as they touched.

I love you.

I've loved you since that first day we met. When I fell into your arms and you surrounded me with your warmth. You are the reason I exist. The reason I go on. The reason I try. You give me hope.

She thought the words as they kissed, heard them reflected back with emotion, strong and pure.

When he lifted his lips, Rianthe let go of his neck, sliding her hands down his shirt. Now, even without the contact, without touching him, he was still there, with her.

Forever.

His single response wrapped itself around her heart as she nodded her head and answered.

Forever.

They would do this. They must. To save Earth was the only way they could be together. Without thought or fear, knowing he was with her, Rianthe turned to stare at the wood of their oak tree. She saw how the colors changed. How a knot darkened in the center until it disappeared into the core of the venerable old tree. How the bark flowed like a charcoal river.

She reached out with both hands and touched the tree. *Help us. We need guidance.* Together, she and

Kaiden pleaded for answers from the very essence of what they were trying to save.

Earth remained silent. Neither did Taegar join them in the *ehwaz*. Instead, they were transported back to the druid's tower.

A dark man with long, flowing white hair turned from the window.

Bhren!

"Students," he said.

Tears stung Rianthe's eyes, no matter the turmoil in their relationship. She'd missed him. Acting without thought, she flung herself into Bhren's arms. He patted her back for a moment, then set her away from him. For the first time that she recalled, his face softened, showing a fondness she'd never known from him. It was fleeting though. The mask, and the master, quickly returned.

"There is little time," he said.

"How do I fix this?" Rianthe said.

Kaiden put a hand on her shoulder. "We. How do *we* fix this?"

Bhren stared at Rianthe. "You know how."

Shaking her head, she tried to refute his words.

"Deep down inside, you know."

"I think—" She hung her head, her voice nothing more than a whisper. "You misplaced your faith in me. I'm not strong enough."

Kaiden squeezed her shoulder.

Bhren lifted her head so she would look at him. "I did not, student. But there are things you must understand."

He touched both their foreheads and they watched a vision unfold in front of them. Bhren, as a much younger man, with the rest of the Guardian druids in Origin cave.

Circling the light of magic so recently released. Such a bright light flowed from Earth. They circled, leaning in, mumbling words too softly to hear.

Then, they were in a new place. A small clearing in the woods. Another group of druids formed a circle around another stream of light emanating from Earth. Again, they chanted. Rianthe could hear the words this time, but she didn't know them. One voice, stronger than the others, drew her.

Father! Tears flowed freely now. Her father looked as he had all those years ago. Young, robust, full of life and magic. Damian Royan led the circle that only wanted to help the magic heal Earth and guide its people into this new evolution.

Next to him, Valena Royan, her mother. Beautiful in her youth, with eyes bluer than the sky. Tevy's eyes.

Damian turned to her. *Daughter. You must act. Quickly.*

"Tell me what to do."

The magic will be hidden. You must find the seal and release it. Only you.

What did he mean?

Damian turned back to the circle, continued chanting, words she now understood. Words of concealment, words of trust and faith in our future. When the words fell off, the druids in the circle held out their hands. One rune for each druid. Her father pricked his finger with a needle, letting his blood drip onto the rune he held.

The emanations of light, the magic Earth had gifted to humankind for healing, dimmed, fading and fading until it almost disappeared.

No! Rianthe screamed the words inside her head.

Please. No. Don't take the magic away.

Her father looked at her. *We do this to save it. To save Earth. To save you.*

All the druids' arms shook with an unseen effort. Damian's face beaded with sweat as they spoke again.

Shattered by darkness the magic vanished.
It lays in wait for one who's banished.
Hidden power will blossom anew.
Only by passing the darkness through.

The runic key ignites the fire
That coupled with the conduit's power
Must send the magic to the white height
Defeating darkness, restoring light.

They chanted the prophecy. No, that wasn't right. They weren't chanting it, at least, not at first. They were creating it.

The vision Bhren showed to Rianthe and Kaiden morphed again. They'd returned to Origin cave. Bhren led the same chant there. The Guardian druids repeated the prophecy, each holding a rune out. Again, the light didn't completely vanish. A trickle remained, though dim compared to before.

Rianthe finally understood. It hadn't been Earth that hid the power to keep it from the Dark druids.

It had been the Guardian druids.

Then they were back in the tower. Back with Bhren as they'd known him. Tears trickled down his face. "All this... All the hard times. The suppressed magic? It's our fault. We did this. We buried the magic."

Rianthe backed away, stunned at the revelation.

"It was our only option," Bhren continued. "The war took a toll on all of us. Dark druids, with Taegar leading, had grown so powerful we could not defeat them. We hoped to hide the magic until one who was stronger than us came along."

Rianthe covered her ears. She didn't want to hear. It wasn't true.

"That one is you, Rianthe Royan," Bhren said. "You are the one."

"I've tried," she repeated. "I don't have the power."

"You do. You must trust in yourself."

"I've tried. Believe me, I've almost died trying. I don't know how to change what I am."

"There is one more thing I must show you," Bhren said, touching their foreheads again.

Rianthe was still in the druid's tower, but now, she was in a corner watching...herself! Kaiden stood beside her as one of the worst days of her life played out again.

"Stand, novitiate."

Her True-Naming. Rianthe squeezed her eyes shut, unwilling to relive that. Not again.

A much more naïve Rianthe stood in front of Bhren, shoulders back, stance proud.

Bhren laid out the white cloth on the table, then opened his rune-bag, chanting the words of divination.

Please, she pleaded. *Don't make me watch this again.*

The old Druid tossed the runes. Rianthe waited for them to seal her fate, but this time, everything happened in slow motion. Bhren mouthed words, chanting as the runes tumbled to the dirt in one pattern, then shifted. She almost didn't catch it, but as Bhren mumbled, they rolled into a different pattern.

Rianthe looked at Bhren, her jaw dropping.

"You changed my True-Naming."

"Yes."

All the pain of that moment washed back through her, almost doubling her over with its ferocity. "You changed my life in that moment."

"I hid you. I had to because I sensed great danger."

Rianthe glared at him. "Hiding. That seems to be what you Guardian druids are best at."

Bhren's mouth tightened. "I made mistakes. *We* made mistakes. There is nothing I can do about that now. Focus, Rianthe. You must let go of your anger so the true magic within you can come forth. You are the conduit. The one who will free Earth's *awen*. Only you can find the seal and bring together humanity and magic, breaking the seal of darkness and letting the light back in."

Let go of her anger? She'd just been tossed back into the heart of the incident that changed her life, her destiny, and filled her with all-consuming doubt for so many years. While her mentor may have manipulated her True-Naming to protect her, that moment had also changed her present, her future, everything.

She'd never trusted herself after that. And she'd run. Left everything she loved. Uja. Tevy. When she'd returned, her brother lay dead. Pain wracked her brain, her body, and her heart.

She'd fought the man sent by Taegar, who'd killed her brother and decimated New Hope. Deakon had been strong, but she'd won the day. Barely. Kaiden, close to mortally injured, had fallen into a dark place from which he'd only narrowly escaped.

She'd fought Taegar both in the *ehwaz* and in reality. And never once bested her.

If she hadn't been wrongly named animal-handler, this might have all been different. Maybe she'd even be stronger now.

"Do you really believe how you were True-Named is holding you back?" Bhren asked. Not waiting for an answer, he continued. "It did not. Your own perception holds you back. What you witnessed, back when you were ten years old, holds you back. You do not trust yourself."

Why would she trust herself? She hadn't been able to help her parents that fateful day all those years ago. Even though her father told her she was the hope of the future, she couldn't save them. That inadequacy haunted her, following her through life in New Hope and beyond. Her True-Naming further eroded her faith in herself.

Bhren was right. It wasn't his fault. Her self-doubt began long before he changed her True-Naming. Was he also right that it was her own perception of herself that was the root cause of her doubt?

She'd barely defeated Deakon, but she *had* beaten him.

Through each vision and test with Taegar she'd gotten stronger until, in this last struggle, she'd immediately thrown up the shield she needed to protect her brother, transporting herself there through the *ehwaz* without even thinking about it. And she'd tapped power she didn't know lay inside her. Out of need. Without thought. She'd simply done it.

Was it that uncomplicated? Had her own lack of faith been all that held her back? Rianthe had to admit the probability. Taking a deep breath, she looked at Bhren. Saw the emotion in his face. The belief in her, the love, the sternness that had helped her get to this point.

"I am sorry for all I have put you through, Rianthe."
He looked at Kaiden. "You too, son. I made you keep
secrets and drove a wedge between you to save you both.
I ask your forgiveness."

Kaiden, who'd remained quiet throughout, stood
with slumped shoulders. Reliving the day of her True-
Naming had been as difficult for him as it was for her.
That day had been tough for both of them. She saw his
struggle now.

New Hope or Rianthe. Make the choice.

Maybe it was even worse for him.

Kaiden gulped and straightened, seemingly releasing
the anger and angst of that day. He held out a hand to
Bhren, who grasped his arm in a brief warrior greeting.
"There is nothing to forgive. You did what you needed to.
Rianthe remains safe, and now, we have a chance to
defeat the darkness for all time. Because of you."

Just like that, he forgave Bhren. If Kaiden, whose
scars were as deep as Rianthe's, found that mercy within
him, maybe she could too.

Bhren turned back to her. "I wish I had been there to
guide you. Maybe things would not be so dire."

"I wouldn't be where I am now if it weren't for the
lessons I learned on my own, but I...I think you're right.
I've been holding myself back this whole time."

"It is time for you to witness the truth of your True-
Naming."

Rianthe turned to the table without reservation.
Bhren picked up the runes, speaking the words over them
once again, then tossed them. This time there was no
hesitation, no shifting of the pattern. Only truth. Even
with the day's revelations, the results astounded her.

"I am not Rianthe. I am not animal handler."

"You are not. You were Rianth. You are now, and forever will be, Erianth. *Sowilo.* The force that will guide us to enlightenment. Strongest of all the druids."

Strongest. Erianth. She didn't know how to feel. Confused, elated, humbled? Yet something deep down felt right. Something inside her coalesced, shutting the door on doubt and her lack of confidence.

Erianth. A name denoting power. A name only she could own. Power, no longer held back by doubt, welled up within her. Power to be called upon in an instant filled her. Rianthe... No. She had a new name now. *I am Erianth.*

You are the hope of the future, daughter. Do not be afraid to find your destiny. Damian Royan's final words came back to her.

Yes. She believed it now. This was who she was meant to be. And now, because of this influx of power and knowledge, she knew how to find the seal and break it open. She called on some of her newfound power to close off this piece of her mind so Kaiden would not be privy to her thoughts.

She turned to the man she loved. "I'm not an animal handler."

Kaiden's grin was wide. "Tevy will be very happy to hear that. I'm glad you've become the person you were meant to be. Now. Forever. You are Erianth. Although, I might have trouble getting used to that name."

The smile hiding beneath her thoughts broke free. "I'm Rianthe as well. I will always be both."

Kaiden touched her cheek. "Erianth or Rianthe, you'll always be my Ri."

"Yes," she said. "Always." She wanted him to remember this moment, to feel her love for him. It would soothe him afterwards. Everything in her life had led up to this point, and she would soon undertake the final test, paying the final price. Erianth would do it gladly, to know her people would survive. Tevy would survive. Kaiden would live, even thrive. They would all find happiness again.

She turned to Bhren. "Thank you for your wisdom," she said, using the phrase she'd learned so well as he'd mentored her.

He acknowledged her gratitude with a nod of his head.

"Will we see you again?" Kaiden asked. "Can we come back here, to this place?"

"I was ancient before the Forever breath left me, with little left to help you. This one vision has taken what is left of my spirit. It is time for me to rest." He'd already grown fainter. "Have faith..." The rest of his words faded along with the vision.

Tears fell from Erianth's and Kaiden's eyes as the vision dissipated, along with their beloved mentor. Soon, everything was gone and Erianth opened her eyes, no longer hugging the tree, but Kaiden.

"It's like losing him all over again," Kaiden whispered.

Erianth took deep breaths, trying to calm herself. With a final squeeze, she let go of Kaiden, stepping back to stretch muscles stiff from being too long in one position. Bhren had helped her one last time. He'd slipped the final piece of information into place, helping her to recognize who and what she was. *Sowilo*. Sunlight. The one who'd gone through darkness now must bring light back to the world. It was time to step into that role for the first, and possibly the last, time.

"Come on. We have to return to New Hope."

"Wait. Your gloves," Kaiden said, picking them up.

Erianth took them and threw them far away. She'd worn them for too many years. "I don't need them anymore."

CHAPTER EIGHTEEN

Erianth could see that Kaiden was confused, hurt maybe, but she didn't have time to give him answers. She was already at the rock wall, surprisingly full of energy, as if the scars of everything that happened to her had disappeared. She was a new person, driven to her mission, and Kaiden had no clue. During the vision they'd shared with Bhren she'd been able to shield her plans to deal with Taegar from him, as well as her plans to find that seal.

"Wait," he said. "Let me go down first." He sped down the wall. "Ri, have a care. You're weak from the coma, and those visions always take something out of you."

"No, I'm not weak." She laughed. How long had it been since she laughed? "I don't feel at all weak. I'm...invigorated. And, I'm ready, Kaiden. I know what I have to do."

He looked doubtful, but he followed her as she raced back to New Hope. The protector. Her protector. She knew he'd give all he had to keep her safe through whatever she'd decided must be done.

Erianth didn't stop until she reached the druid's tower where Tevy waited near the door. She'd known he would be there. Kaiden seemed shocked by her lack of surprise. Obviously, he hadn't known, and the worry lines on his face deepened. They were connected on so many levels, yet she had to leave him in the dark. Shut him out. It hurt her, but he couldn't know what she had planned.

"You know what I have to do," she said to Tevy.

"I sensed your need. I am here for you, sister. Erianth," he replied.

"Wait, how does he know and I don't?" Kaiden came up beside them. He'd been hard-pressed to keep up with her during the race back to the tower, and Erianth hoped it lent credence to her magical recovery. She'd never run that fast in her life.

"I understand now, Kaiden. I understand everything. I'm sorry, but there's no time to explain," she said.

Tevy nodded. "There's little time to waste."

He was right. In the short time she and Kaiden had been gone, a blanket had been tossed over the sun. Everything had darkened.

"You don't have the runes," Tevy said.

"Don't worry, little brother. I've got this."

Kaiden protested, his face a wash of confusion.

"I'm sorry. There's no time," Erianth said. "Tevy, I need all the Royan strength."

"I'll be here," Tevy said. "The wolves, too. You have the animals' strength."

"I feel it. Their energy, joined with mine," she said, soaking in adrenaline. "Thank you. And be safe, Tevy." Erianth brushed away her fear of what Tevy's life would become if she failed. She must not fail. She would not. She turned to run her hands over the *awen* symbol inscribed in the rock beside the tower door. The carved symbol had reappeared on its own once the tower walls had gone up. Now, it pulsed with a light that cut through the growing darkness. The same symbol had adorned the original tower, and was also carved into the rock outside Origin cave. Erianth knew that the sign lay embedded in the rock outside Taegar's lair, too. The sign of the *awen*. Earth's spirit.

"Wait!" Fraka hollered from the back of the growing crowd outside the tower. She rushed forward, six-month-old Ujami in her arms. "He's been crying for half an hour. Saying 'Eri, Eri.' He didn't stop until I raced over here."

Erianth took her nephew from Fraka. He calmed as soon as she held him. The boy's eyes were red-rimmed but clear as he looked at her. He was so much like his father. He placed a chubby hand on either side of Erianth's face, staring at her with the eyes of a wise man. "Wif' you. Plants."

"What's he saying?" Fraka asked. "I don't understand."

"I understand him perfectly," Erianth said as a second rush of energy filled her. "Do not deplete yourself," she whispered to the boy, who should not be able to understand, but did. "I need you to live, to thrive, to carry on your father's vision." She kissed Ujami's forehead before handing him back to his mother.

Somehow, word had spread and the entire village

gathered around the tower. Erianth didn't have time to explain to them, but she took a precious moment to look over the faces of her friends. Her family. New Hope.

"It's time," she said, then turned and walked into the tower.

Kaiden followed her, but she stopped him with a hand to his chest. "You cannot help with this."

I understand none of this, Kaiden mind-spoke. *But I am* thurisaz. *I am protector. I offer you my strength.*

No words need be spoken between them anymore. They were bonded on a much deeper level. On a magical level.

Erianth cupped his cheek. *I'm sorry. You cannot help me with this journey, no matter how much you wish to.*

He clutched her hand. *I can't protect you from here.*

You will have to. Erianth kissed him. "I love you, Kaiden Darcy. I always have." She pulled her hand free.

"You sound like you're saying goodbye."

The smile she wanted to give him remained hidden. She didn't dare answer his unspoken question. She must see this through. There were no more words to say. With one last look around, she closed the door and climbed the stairs to the tower room.

She didn't give herself time to think. Walking straight up to the table in the center, she plunged her hands into its square of dirt. Dirt she now knew covered up the secret Bhren had held for over one hundred years. Dirt that capped the final place the magic had been stifled to end the Great Magic War. This tower was built on the very spot her father, Damian Royan, had stood all those years ago, uttering the chant he'd created. The prophecy that Erianth finally understood.

Three points of magical origin were marked with the

symbol of the *awen,* Earth's spirit. The symbol meant to show the way, only she'd never realized it until now. Everything must unify and work together. Ujami for the plants. Tevy for the animals. And she was Earth and the sun, the channel through which the magic flowed. To release the *awen,* she must find it here. Find the magic, pull the threads together, intertwine them, then bind the magic to Earth for all time, never to be used for dark purposes again.

To pull the magic to her, she needed the talisman.

With her hands deep in the soil, Erianth called the magic. A tingle started, first in her fingertips, then in her wrists and arms, finally filling her. The power consumed her, the warmth turning to heat. The room brightened with her glow as she emanated power. Just like Taegar had when she'd been in direct contact with the magic. Except there was no discord. Here, the power was only pure, only white.

Beautiful magic.

Healing magic.

Erianth dug deeper into Earth's core, found the path that led to the seal the Guardian druids had put upon the *awen,* and heard the whispers of her father's voice and the others from all those years ago. They had forced the magic back, deep into the center of their world, to protect it. She must open that portal.

At the edge of her vision, something moved. Something dark and sinister grew, joining her, trying to push her back.

Taegar.

The magic is mine, she shouted.

It belongs to Earth. You shall never have it.

Taegar came at her with a fury before unseen, arms

reaching out, hands ready to grasp the runes around Erianth's neck.

The force of their connection threw them both back. Erianth hit the floor hard, pain intensifying as the air whooshed out of her lungs. Suddenly, they were both there, in the tower. No vision, no *ehwaz*. A real-time battle.

Leaping to her feet, Erianth pushed the pain away and put the table between them. Taegar stood on the opposite side. She straightened, grew taller, glowing brilliant gold.

I will have the runes, little one. One way or the other.

Erianth glanced down, surprised that her own body shone with a similar light. Untainted white light. Earth light. Power coursed through her, growing and growing as she looked again at Taegar.

I choose the other.

Taegar came at her in an instant, fire flying from her fingers.

Erianth threw up a shield and the flames bounced off.

Next came bolts of lightning, screaming toward her at incredible speeds, one after another with no pause. Erianth's shield continued to protect her. Taegar rounded the table, advancing on her. Bony hands pounded the shield, trying to break it.

The shield held. Still, Erianth saw no end to this. She must somehow finish Taegar and gain the talisman.

She was *sowilo*, the magnet that drew all the energy. Was it that simple? Erianth looked at Taegar, the Dark druid's golden eyes now glowing red with fury.

"I am Erianth," she said. "I am *sowilo*. I am Earth. I

am everything."

The golden eyes in the glow that was Earth's nemesis widened, and she redoubled her efforts to get through the shield.

Absorb, Erianth told her shield. Nothing happened. Taegar continued to pound away at her with any element available. Fist, fire, and air. *Absorb,* Erianth whispered again. Slowly, almost imperceptibly, the pounding lessened. Erianth's shield grew brighter, no longer repelling the energy thrown at it, but pulling it in, strengthening with each bolt or flame.

Erianth pushed against Taegar, who retreated a step. She pushed again, and again. She kept at it until Taegar had been backed against the wall.

The light surrounding Taegar dimmed and the soulless eyes grew round. Erianth saw the Dark druid's final attempt coming. A tendril of magic tried to slip underneath the shield. Erianth stepped on it, and it withered to nothing but ash.

"Your time is at an end," she said to Taegar. "I am Erianth. It is humanity's time now."

"Noooooo," Taegar screamed, renewing her efforts. Every part of her burned bright once again. Then, so slowly Erianth didn't notice at first, the radiance around her lessened. The *awen* deserted her. All light, all presence left her body and she slumped to the floor.

Erianth had done it. She had defeated Taegar. She should be ecstatic, but she felt no euphoria. To lose someone so potent in their ability seemed such a waste. Erianth let her shield go and knelt beside Taegar, whose broken strength was no longer a danger. A lifetime of pain filled the dimming eyes. The shell Taegar had become, the things she had done, did not define the early druid, so full of wonder and life. Sadness filled Erianth for what Taegar had become. She placed a hand on the robe. "Your time is at an end. The age of Earth is begun. Be at peace."

Red eyes turned golden one last time, then dimmed until the spark of life left her. Soon her form glowed anew, but this was a glow Erianth knew and welcomed. As she watched, what remained of Taegar turned to ash. A sigh filled the room, blowing the ash up and away.

Erianth stood there for a long time, still aglow, awash in power, unable to reconcile the fact that the druid who'd all but destroyed Earth had been conquered. By her. As a village and beyond, they'd worked so hard and so long for this moment. She glanced around, wanting to share it, but no one was there because she'd chosen not to endanger the people she loved. This was meant to be a solitary journey. She hoped they would know, when she was gone, that she'd destroyed Taegar. That they would rebuild their lives and go forward in happiness.

Nothing remained of Taegar but the runes. Erianth picked them up, poured the others from her bag, and stared at them. Together again. Her father's last gift to her, and to the world.

The ground beneath Erianth shook, reminding her that only part of the prophecy had been fulfilled. She turned to the table. Runes clasped in hand, she dug deep into the soil. She began to chant.

"I am Erianth Royan, daughter of Damian Royan. I have been shattered by darkness and have passed through to the light. I am the carrier of Royan magic, the catalyst, the conduit. I hold the runic key. You must obey. Release!"

She said the words over and over again, pouring all

of herself into her effort to free the *awen*. Heart and soul gave everything of themselves. Earth bucked, then steadied, yet there was no outpouring of light.

Erianth called up more magic, including the touch of animal and plant within her, and held her hands firmly in the soil, reaching deep. Browns and grays and blacks became dwindled rivers of life-giving water, then rock. Precious minerals and gems gave way as she found Earth's centric molten lava, where she grasped again for the magical seal, a knotted thread of light that that roared through the magma below, but dwindled to nothing above the tangle where the knot was tied off, guarding the power and keeping the *awen* captive.

Repeating the chant until she went hoarse, Erianth poured her soul into the heat. The room brightened further as she spoke. She was *sowilo*. She was the light who had been banished and passed through the darkness. She was the prophesied one.

Release, she commanded again. She held the runes further under the dirt, calling the knot to unravel and come to her.

With no warning, the seal burst apart in a shower of sparks. The knot untangled and the thread of magic poured forth, up, up up. Filling her, filling Earth's layers, its crust, and finally, bursting through the thatched roof and into the sky.

So much magic, Erianth could hardly stand it. It filled her, consumed her. She fought to remember she had not completed her quest. Reaching further, she called the magic from the cave Taegar had used, and from Origin cave. She twined the strands together into one whole filament – one strong, unknotted cord. She chanted again, even as the magic took everything she had.

Where once the magic was gifted to humankind.
Now it belongs to Earth.
Forever bound, forever freed.

The words came unbidden as the *awen* poured forth. No more darkness. Only pure, white goodness remained in the magic.

Thank you. The words came to her, whispered on air.

Erianth barely heard them. She grew weaker as the magic grew stronger. She'd given everything she had of herself to bind the magic so no one could use it for themselves ever again. Earth would hold control from this day forward.

What she'd done alone, it had once taken an entire circle of druids to do.

Earth, humanity, animal, plant. All would be free. They would live, thrive. Tevy, Kaiden, everyone's life would be better.

To make that happen, she must succumb.

So be it.

Erianth screamed, letting her voice give the last of herself.

CHAPTER NINETEEN

Kaiden stared up at the darkened window. No sound, no nothing. What was happening? He'd tried the door after it had closed behind Ri, but it wouldn't open. He pounded on the door, calling upon all of his strength to open it, to no avail. Then he prayed to Earth to help him, to let him help her.

She planned to do this herself. That scared him worse than anything ever had.

Lights flickered, then grew in the window. Everyone gathered there watched as the light grew brighter and brighter. Then, a crash. No screams, no cry from Erianth, but a frantic noise, like books and furniture being thrown.

Kaiden yanked again at the door. "Ri, let me in," he shouted. "I can help. I have to help."

Suddenly, the light disappeared and darkness claimed his vision. Dram, but he needed to get in there.

When the light reappeared in the window, he hit the

door with his shoulder, again and again, trying to break it down. *Ri, please. Let me in. Why are you doing this alone?*

That no answer came flash-froze his heart.

Roulf joined Kaiden. "I don't know much from my training all those years ago, but I know this. Erianth must somehow find the seal and break it, then bind the magic to Earth so no one can tamper with it ever again. To do that, no one else can be there. It must only be her and Earth. Alone. Trusting each other. Believing in each other. Only one can own the power. Only she can bind it."

Panic filled Kaiden. "You told her to be careful. That the magic will use her up."

Sadness filled Roulf's eyes. "I did. That's...still possible, even though she has come into her powers."

"No!" Kaiden shouted. Erianth's screams reached him at the same time.

"We have to help her!"

Roulf shook his head. "I don't know how."

Kaiden took in the entire village of New Hope as they stood there watching the light with wonder and fear in their eyes. A village that Bhren had brought together for one purpose. To help release the magic and heal Earth. Bhren had believed in them, giving them the great purpose of helping the prophesied one bring the light back. Maybe they were there for another purpose. Maybe they were there to save Erianth.

"Everyone," he shouted. "Come here!"

They looked at him slowly, as if coming out of a trance.

"Hold hands. This will take all of us. Encircle the tower. Ri needs us. We need to give her our strength, our magic, anything we can to keep her from losing herself in this battle."

Tevy grabbed his hand. Fraka, Jonah, Raisa, Mokie, Anniah. Everyone joined hands until there was one unbroken circle surrounding the druid's tower.

"Rianthe is now Erianth, *sowilo*, prophesied one," Kaiden said. "Focus on her. Send her your thoughts, your magic, your love. Give her the strength to live through what she is doing. Concentrate only on her. On Erianth. Our salvation."

They turned their faces toward the beams of light coming from the tower window. Kaiden did the same, cocooned in the warming love and energy of his fellow villagers. A glow encompassed the circle of people. A glow of hope.

A new circle of Guardian druids had just been born, with Erianth to lead them. Kaiden knew in his heart this was meant to be. This was what they'd been brought together to do. To become. This was how they would keep Erianth from losing herself to the magic.

It had to be. Otherwise, there was no purpose.

He stared at the windows. Gave all his love, all his power, to her. He let it flow through the bond, his energy and that of the others. Together, they pooled their magic and sent it forth through him. Up, up, up, into the tower room. To Erianth.

Live, Ri. For us. For me. Please.

CHAPTER TWENTY

Warmth surrounded Erianth. Softness below and above her. Light filtered through her eyelids. She didn't open them. Not yet. She was too comfortable and having the loveliest dream.

They were in their spot, above their beautiful lake, leaning against their tree. She was in Kaiden's arms. The trees were lush with green needles and budding leaves. Foliage grew all around them, dense and dark and rich with nutrients. Flowers blossomed and birds sang. Bees raced from flower to flower, feeding off the sweet nectar in the plants.

She wanted to stay here forever. In Kaiden's arms.

Then, the memories flooded back. She was Rianthe no longer. She'd become Erianth. It all came back to her. Taegar, the light, releasing the magic, giving it back to Earth. And losing herself in the process. This must be Earth's final gift to her. Peace and comfort.

Erianth smiled.

"Wake up, sleepyhead."

Kaiden? It was his voice, but how could he be here? Unless—

Erianth opened her eyes and blinked. It didn't feel like she was in some afterlife. Instead, she lay in the tower. In her bed. With sunlight, almost blinding sunlight, streaming through the window. And Kaiden, sitting there smiling on the edge of her bed.

Her heart soared at the sight of him.

"It's about time you woke up."

"How—" Her voice croaked as if she hadn't used it in quite a while.

"Shhh. Questions later. For now, see if you can drink this tea. I've been dribbling it into your mouth long enough. It's time you made my life easier."

Erianth sat up a little, with Kaiden's help, and sipped the tea. The warm liquid soothed her parched throat. When she'd finished it, she sat up the rest of the way. Kaiden packed pillows in behind her and she leaned against them, grateful for the support.

"How long have I been here? What happened? How am I here?"

"Over a week. You seem to hibernate when you need to heal from something. It's pretty scary, to be honest."

She looked at him, saw the dark circles under his eyes, even if they were alight with joy. "You look like you haven't slept in days."

"I have. Off and on. Mother made me."

A cot lay empty in the corner. He'd been here with her the whole time. Erianth knew it. Because she'd do the same for him. Had, in fact, after Deakon had injured him so badly.

"Earth?"

Kaiden's smile widened. "Earth is on its way to healing. Already, most of the spoilage from Taegar's last attempt to destroy us has disappeared. Thanks to you."

Taegar.

"She's gone."

"We know. The darkness has disappeared. The light has returned."

Tevy loped in, shifting back to his human form as he did so. "Good day, Rianthe," he said, pulling on pants that lay on the cot and settling on the other side of her bed. "Or, Erianth, as I guess I'd better get used to calling you now." He giggled. Actually giggled. This was the Tevy she'd known all his life.

Erianth hugged him. "It's good to see you smile."

"There's more to smile about. Wait 'til you see. You did it. You really did it!"

"We did it, dearest brother. I felt you with me. I felt your energy." She grabbed his hand, then Kaiden's. "All of you. I remember now. You somehow kept me from...disappearing."

"And you saved us all," Kaiden said, squeezing her hand in turn.

"You have *got* to see the changes, Sis." Tevy rose and tugged on her arm, ready to haul her outside to show her.

"Wait a minute," she said with a laugh. "Give me a minute to get my legs underneath me."

"Awww. All right, but don't take too long. I'll be outside. In the sunshine!" He bounded out without waiting for a response.

"Since when," Kaiden said, "do you exercise caution when it comes to your own well-being?"

"I didn't expect to be alive after everything. Now that I am, I fully plan to stick around and enjoy it." With the imminent danger gone, she wanted more joy in her life.

We are joyful because of you, Taschia mind-spoke, plodding in to rub against Erianth. *It is good to see you awake, sister.*

"It's good to *be* awake." Erianth laughed. It really did feel good. So good, in fact, she stood up, with Kaiden's arm for support. She found herself quite able to walk around the room, surprised she wasn't weaker.

You have Kai-den to thank.

Erianth gazed at Kaiden. His grin hadn't disappeared since she'd opened her eyes. When was the last time she'd seen him this happy? It had been a long, long time. He looked good this way. Really good. Like all the stress of the last few years had fallen away. He even looked younger.

"Taschia says I have you to thank for my energy. Probably for my life, if the pride in your expression is any indication."

He nodded. "We banded together. All of New Hope circled the tower while you were inside. We couldn't be with you for what you needed to do. I understand that now. But we tried to give you enough energy to keep you grounded, so you wouldn't be lost to the magic."

One big circle, all holding hands. Our pack stood with this circle. Our energy helped as well.

"One big circle." Erianth canted her head. "Like a druid's circle. I think you may have just described the newest iteration of the Guardian circle of druids."

"I think you're right," Roulf said, joining them. "An entire village of Guardian druids, keeping watch over the magic and humankind, continuing to guide all to a co-existent life in this new evolution." He hugged Erianth. "It's good to see you up, child."

Erianth returned his hug. "I'm glad you're still here."

"I've grown somewhat accustomed to the people of New Hope. I might just have to stick around." He shrugged. "For a while, I mean. I had thought to revisit Origin cave, now that it's safe. I'd like to see if I can bring your parents book back here."

"I'd like that, too." Erianth said, hugging him again.

They walked out of the druid's tower together, Taschia beside them. The sunlight was so bright, Erianth shielded her eyes for a moment. When they adjusted, the changes astonished her. They were nothing short of miraculous. The world had made an almost complete turnaround while she'd slept.

Earth had come to life. The trees were no longer gnarled, black, decomposing posts. They'd grown tall again. Taegar's poisonous blight had been reversed. They weren't yet normal, but new shoots of life burst from them.

On the ground, light green sprouts of grass grew everywhere. The smell of decay had fled. And the weather! It had turned from winter to spring overnight, it seemed. It was hard to believe.

"It gets even better," Kaiden said, holding out his arm. "Up for a little walk?"

"You bet," she said, taking his arm. Not because she needed to, but because there was no place she wanted to be more than at Kaiden's side. Her insides fluttered, just as they had all those years ago. Even at ten years old, she'd known she was meant to be with Kaiden. Her heart, overflowing with joy and love, lightened until any remaining burden disappearing. For the first time, she could be carefree. Tears of happiness stung her eyes as she gazed at Kaiden's smiling face.

Tevy's wolves showed up, dancing and prancing in front of the pair as they walked.

They are happy you are so well, Taschia said.

Thank them for me. Tell them I am happy, too.

They entered the growing hut and Erianth was amazed again. Plants, herbs, everything was lush and looked like it had been growing for weeks, not just a few days. Fraka stood in the middle of it all with Ujami on her hip.

"Good day, Ri—Erianth." Fraka gave her a one-armed hug. "It's great to see you up. And healthy. You look like years have fallen off you."

"Thank you," Erianth said, blushing at a compliment she wasn't used to hearing.

"Isn't this great?" Fraka waved her arm around the room.

"It's wonderful."

"And look at this." She pulled a seedling close. Ujami touched it and it shot up about two inches.

Erianth's mouth hung open. "How can he do that?"

"It's the magic."

"I bound the magic to Earth. I didn't think any part of the *awen* would be left for us."

"Whatever you did, however you did it, all our abilities have grown. We have more ability now than we ever have. Except maybe back before the Great Magic War," Fraka said.

"It's true," Kaiden said. "Raisa's arm was healed by her own magic. Anniah and Kathra are cooking up huge meals in half the time. Even my own ability to protect...well, it may not be as necessary now, but I'm stronger than ever. I feel like I could take on anything and win."

"Maybe," Erianth said slowly, "Earth gifted us part of its *awen* as a thank you."

Kaiden nodded. "We could chat on and on about the changes, but there are others who want to thank you."

He led her out of the growing hut and they went next door to the dining and kitchen hall. The rebuilding had sped along, and the longhouse was almost completely roofed in.

"I thought you might want something solid to eat. You've had nothing but mother's tea for days."

On cue, Erianth's stomach growled. She nodded, laughing. Anniah saw her from the other side of the room and squealed, racing to her and hugging her so tight Erianth thought she might break apart.

"Thank you, thank you, thank you," Anniah said. "You've given us back our lives. She clutched her stomach, which was just starting to show the growing baby inside. Tears filled her eyes. "You've given us all a new chance at life."

"It wasn't just me. I've been told I got a lot of help. I think—" Erianth laid a hand on Anniah's stomach, "you and your son were part of what kept me alive."

Anniah's eyes grew wide. "A son?"

"A son," Erianth confirmed, surprised she'd detected that. Maybe that prescience was part of her own enhanced magical ability. She raised her hands and wiggled her fingers. "I don't have gloves on."

Kaiden grabbed her hand. *You won't ever need to wear them again. Anything you touch, or sense, will be filled with goodness from now on.*

"I hope you don't mind knowing you're having a son," she said to her friend.

"Not at all." Anniah squealed again. "I have to go tell Mokie. He's in the growing fields." She ran off without waiting for a response.

Kathra, who'd come up behind them, set down a plate of stew. "This should help your stomach start off," she said, indicating Erianth should sit.

She did, grateful for it. Her energy was flagging. The stew looked rich, with thick sauce and filled with vegetables. The first bite almost melted in her mouth. Erianth looked up at Kathra, whose smile filled the room with sunshine.

"The growing fields, it's like they regenerated. Everything is growing. And the root vegetables beneath the surface never got touched by the blight. We have food. Enough to feed everyone."

"The animals are returning, as well. And we've begun hearing news from other settlements," Jonah said, giving Erianth a hug as he and Raisa joined them. Her hug followed on the heels of her husband's. "It's not just us. It's everywhere. Earth is healing itself, thanks to you."

Tears blurred Erianth's eyes. "It's just so hard to believe it's done."

Raisa looked younger, more youthful than when Erianth had last she'd seen her. Was Earth reversing the aging process, too?

"We've all felt an influx of energy. Not just the plants. You've brought us back from the brink of destruction, Erianth Royan." Jonah put a hand on her shoulder and squeezed. "Thank you doesn't seem like enough."

Erianth shook her head. "It was everyone—"

"No," Jonah said. "There will be no modesty in this. *You* did it. *You* fulfilled the prophecy."

"And you all kept me alive." Her voice broke. "I think we're even."

Raisa clasped both of Erianth's hands for a quick moment. "You are as important to us as Earth is. But look around. Everything's changed."

"We have hope because of you," Jonah said.

"Yep," Mokie said from the outskirts of the little group as he joined them, Anniah beside him. "But don't expect me to get used to that new name of yours anytime soon. You'll always be Rianthe to me."

"And Ri to me," Kaiden whispered in her ear.

Erianth hugged him tight. She didn't try to stop the healing tears that flowed down her face. She wasn't the only one crying. Most of the village stopped by, thanking her with their own tears of gratitude. They'd fought so hard for so long. She found it hard to believe it was really over. That she could be happy. That she could love and be loved.

Erianth looked at Kaiden, saw the love in his eyes.

And she believed.

~~~

Later that day, Kaiden helped her climb up to the place she'd always been most at home. The woods above the lake showed life and growth and would soon return to their former glory. The lake itself looked almost devoid of algae, cleansed by the sunshine.

"The fish will come back soon. I'm certain of it," Kaiden said.

Erianth didn't want to think about fish. For now, it felt good just to lay there, against their tree, watching
~~~

their lake. From within Kaiden's arms. "I dreamed about this as I was waking up."

"And I prayed continually for the day we could be here. You and me, together. I love you," he said.

"I love you, too."

"I think," Kaiden pulled her tighter into his embrace, "we can finally just be ourselves."

"And maybe we can be a little selfish, for a while."

He kissed her. A kiss long with love. With promise. With hope. A kiss heartily returned.

"I love your hair," Kaiden said as he wound a tendril around his finger.

"I know," she said with a laugh.

"I'm glad you grew it back."

"I cut it to wipe away my past."

"A hurtful past I helped create."

Erianth curled tighter against him. "We're pretty well done with that. Although, if I managed to beat you on the training fields, I might be able to finally lay it all to rest."

"Never," he said, his mock-angry voice laced with humor. "I will always be Almighty Kaiden to you."

She smiled at the moniker he'd forced her to say each time he'd beat her in practice. "Yes," she said truthfully. "You always will be that to me."

There were things to do, plans to make, a future to settle into. But all that could wait. For now, it was enough to be in Kaiden's arms.

EPILOGUE

"Use your magic, Ri. Please. It will lessen the pain." Worry and tension clutched Kaiden's jaw and wrinkled his brow, his green eyes wide with concern as he held her.

Erianth refused to use the magic. Earth had gifted strong magic to those with an inclination toward it. They'd decided as a whole that it shouldn't be used for selfish purposes, but for the greater good. That message rippled through the healing Earth without argument. She touched her mate's cheek. "I want to feel this. I want to know every moment of the joy and pain of her birth."

She bit down on her lip as the throbbing ripped through her again, trying not to cry out.

"Push," Raisa said. "It's time. Push with everything you've got."

Kaiden raised her and Erianth grunted as she bore down one final time and pushed the babe from her. She crumpled back onto the bed, panting with exhaustion after hours of laboring. Kaiden stroked her hair, still worried. He always worried, her husband.

Raisa held the now swaddled babe out to Kaiden. "Your beautiful daughter," she said turning as soon as the babe was settled in his arms, leaving them alone with their newling.

Kaiden stared at the babe for a long time, unmoving. Erianth grew anxious for a glimpse of her daughter and held out her arms. Kaiden kissed the babe's forehead, then turned to Erianth. There were tears in his eyes.

"How can she be so beautiful?" he asked.

Erianth took her. "She's the most beautiful newling I've ever seen." Wonder filled her that this tiny creature, who looked up at them with such trust in her eyes, had come from them.

"I think we should name her Valena," Kaiden said.

Erianth smiled her agreement through tears, overwhelmed at his honor to her mother's memory. "She will be a healer, like Raisa, and like her grandmother."

Kaiden knelt beside Erianth. They could not stop staring at what they'd created.

"Look at her," she said. "She's perfect in every way." Erianth touched Kaiden's cheek again and he covered her hand, as together, they held the babe.

"Thank you," he said.

"Earth's bounty has blessed us."

"That it has," he agreed, leaning in to kiss her.

Little Valena stared at them with wide, intelligent eyes.

"I think she'll have your eyes, Kaiden. The color of our lake."

"And she'll have your soft, dark, beautiful hair."

Kaiden wound a strand around his finger. "And your power."

"If Ujami is any indication of the power in this next generation, she'll definitely be more magical than I am."

Valena held up a fist. Erianth touched it, then Kaiden, forming a trilogy of love. The babe's fingers began to glow, her warmth spreading out to Erianth and Kaiden, forming a bond that would never be torn apart.

Erianth pulled back the blanket for a closer look at their daughter. She counted toes, jiggled her round little belly, and ran her hand over Valena's head of fuzz. The babe, who hadn't cried yet, sighed in contentment then turned toward her mother in search of food.

The new parents both stared at their baby in wonder, then turned to each other.

"Her ears are pointed," they said in unison.
The end.

Thank you for reading **Birthright**, the final story in the Earth Legacy series. If you enjoyed this book, please consider leaving a review wherever you prefer, and know that it would be greatly appreciated. And keep your eye out for more stories in the this world. Coming soon: **Awakening**, the prequel to the Great Magic War.

For new release information and news about Laurie Ryan, please join her newsletter.

AUTHOR'S NOTE AND ACKNOWLEDGEMENTS

It's always bittersweet, closing the book on a story that ends a world I've spent so much time in. This one is even tougher since the seeds of this story have been with me since my teen years. There will be other stories in this world. A prequel, Tevy's story, and another series set after this one. So in some ways, it's easier for me to say goodbye to beloved characters, since you and I will see some of them again.

The premises of most of my stories center around the belief that it takes a village to get things accomplished. This series has proven that over and over again. From critique partners who see the holes I cannot, to the editor who makes me shine. From the cover artist who sees my vision better than I do to the beta readers who give me hope there will be a place for this story to thrive. I appreciate all of you more than I can say.

But most of all, I want to thank Ron and Chris, brothers extraordinaire. We shared our love of Tolkien from the first reading of the hobbit to the tenth, and eleventh (or should I say elevenses.) You kept my love of alternate worlds strong and gave me the motivation to write these stories.

I strove to pay homage to druid beliefs in this story because of their unfailing love and respect for nature. While most of the terms in this story are runic in nature, I chose the druid term *awen* to represent Earth's magic. It translates as something like flowing spirit or inspiration. It felt completely right for this series, which is all about listening to the earth as it tries to help us all find a way to survive.

I believe we are near the point where drastic changes will be needed to ensure the continued existence of future generations. This story, this series, comes out of that belief. I hope you enjoyed it.

Thank you.

BOOKLIST

Fantasy by Laurie Ryan
Survival
Enlightenment
Birthright

Contemporary romance stories by Laurie Ryan
Tropical Persuasions Series
Stolen Treasures
Pirate's Promise
Dare To Love

Standalone
Northern Lights
Healing Love
(also part of the Holiday Magic anthology)
Lost and Found

Women's Fiction by Laurie Ryan
Show Me

ABOUT THE AUTHOR

Laurie Ryan writes fantasy and contemporary romance. Growing up a devoted reader, Laurie Ryan immersed herself in the diverse works of authors like Tolkien and Woodiwiss. She is passionate about every aspect of a book: beginning, middle, and end. She can't arrive to a movie five minutes late, has never been able to read the end of a book before the beginning, and is a strong believer in reading the book before seeing the movie.

Laurie lives in the beautiful Pacific Northwest, in the shadow of Mt. Rainier and a short drive to beach-walking next to the Pacific Ocean, with her handsome, he-can-fix-anything husband and their gray, seventeen-pound cat, Dude.

www.laurieryanauthor.com

A sneak peek at the coming Earth Legacy prequel...

AWAKENING
(Prequel to the Earth Legacy series)

CHAPTER ONE

Damian Royan stood on the promontory and stared out over the lake, enjoying a warmer than usual day for mid-September. Nearby, the organized chaos of visitors who'd come to see the carved faces of Mt. Rushmore, would soon begin. Here, though, serene water reflected majestic evergreens reaching for the scattered clouds in an otherwise cerulean sky, a stark contrast to Damian's mood. If what he'd heard held any truth, this peaceful place would soon be disturbed. No, not disturbed. Non-existent. All of this sacred beauty—gone. Sold to the highest bidder. The idea was unconscionable. How could anyone destroy this?

A warm breeze lifted the hair off his shoulders with gentle abandon. Birds still sang their morning songs. A fish leaped from the water, daring a hawk to try catching him. Accepting the challenge, the hawk dove with reckless speed, braking at the last moment to dip talons below the glassy surface and coming up with the arrogant fish in its claws. Wings back-stroked to grab air as the hawk drifted higher and higher with his breakfast.

Even the green grass beneath Damian's feet spoke of rejuvenation and renewal, though Spring lay several months behind them. This was a special place. A sacred place. With closed eyes, Damian prayed to the world around him. This new threat was beyond anything he'd ever dealt with. He needed guidance. Advice on how to placate the threat to everything he held dear. Everything that all of humanity should consider important.

Pebbles trickled down the rock wall to his left and Damian grinned as the dark-haired, blue-eyed reason for his existence appeared and his wife joined him.

"I knew I'd find you here." Valena said, wrapping her arms around his waist. She gazed out over the water and, for a while, they simply enjoyed the moment. The harmonious connection with each other and everything surrounding them. A moment of tranquility. How long would they have this? Damian sighed.

"You seem troubled."

Damian welcomed her embrace and returned it, leaning down to place a kiss on hair that fell to her waist. He loved these mornings, before her hair became confined in the braid that made living outdoors tolerable. His wife only stood as tall as his shoulders, but her diminutive stature ended there. In all other aspects, she was a force to be reckoned with. A strong partner, a loving wife, and a follower of the same beliefs as his.

The druid way. Harmony with the earth and awe for the living world that surrounded and nourished them.

Damian frowned. How long could earth withstand the over-exploitation that reduced it to a commodity?

"What worries you?" Valena asked.

Everything. Damian took a deep breath, letting nature's perfume calm him. To put voice to his concerns lent them credence. Made the possibilities real. Yet this was not a burden he should carry alone.

"Does this have anything to do with the letter Wyeth brought in with the supplies yesterday?"

"Yes. It seems this land has been sold."

Valena turned to look at him. "That can't be. This is government land. Plus, it's a national park."

"Nevertheless, it has been sold. Somehow."

"To whom?"

"A Gordon Darcy." Damian gestured to the computer atop a canvas bag on the grass. "It didn't take much research for this news to become concerning."

"Who is he?"

"A man who buys and sells based on his own whims. He's into everything. Stocks, real estate, gold, oil, minerals." That last option worried Damian the most.

"Even if Gordon Darcy has somehow convinced the government to sell him this land, they would never release mineral rights to him," Valena said.

Damian reached down and picked up the letter from an attorney friend living in D.C.

Valena took the letter from him and scanned it, her fingers tightening on the paper as she read. Done, she looked up at him with tears in her blue eyes. "How did this happen? How can they do this?"

"I don't know, but we have to fight it."

"Agreed. We need to talk with everyone, make the decision together."

Damian nodded, placing his things in the bag and slinging it over his shoulder while he slipped his sandals on. He climbed down first, then reached up to help Valena, who batted his arm away. "How many times have I found you here, deep in thought?"

"A few," Damian said with a laugh.

"Yes." She jumped the last foot to land on both feet. "We even planted one of your favorite oak trees just so you'd have one here. I think I can manage to get up and down a six-foot rock wall."

"I know you can." Damian kissed her. "You are precious to me, my love. So if I get overly protective, you must forgive me."

Valena twined her arms around Damian's neck, kissing him again. "There's nothing to forgive."

Arm in arm, they walked the path back to the tent sites they shared with their friends. As a group, they performed duties as campground hosts. An R.V. sat at the entrance to the park and they each took turns manning it. The truck, their only transportation, sat beside it, unused except for runs into Rapid City to stock up on supplies. Though other campers came with their modern conveniences, Damian, Valena, and their friends preferred a simpler way of life.

Their homes, canvas tents, sat in the more rustic, walk-in sites near the lake. With few amenities, they'd made arrangements with a local hotel for showers, trading landscaping and maintenance. All in all, they had everything they needed. Granted long-term rental of their sites, they acted as caretakers of the campground and surrounding land. This had been a co-existent life that had worked well for several years. Now, it seemed, they were about to lose their home, and so much more.

It didn't take Damian and Valena long to get back to their communal home. At the moment, seven of them lived in five sites, right near the water.

Bhren, his bound white hair a stark contrast to his dark skin, stood in their outdoor kitchen stirring a pot of something smelling very much like apples and cinnamon. He'd drawn breakfast duty this morning. That meant oatmeal, about all the man knew how to cook. Damian laughed, joining him.

"I'm a scholar, not a cook," Bhren grumbled.

"Then why do you always get breakfast duty?" Damian clapped him on the back, then plugged in the laptop to charge. "Seems like a scholar could figure his way out of this predicament."

"I'm being set up."

Bhren's glare held more smoke than fire. For the most part, everyone got along and everyone did their part.

Damian left Bhren to his oatmeal and sat down at the table, watching Valena and Gwen put the finishing touches on a fruit salad. Gwen's husband, Wyeth, set out dishes, bowls, and silverware. Off to the side, waiting for the dish duty she always took on, the perennially happy Taegar sat weaving daisies into a crown of leaves for her head, smiling as she worked. When she'd shown up a year earlier, a young woman in a world of emotional pain, she'd wholeheartedly adopted their simple lifestyle. She was young and had refused to talk about her life before joining them. No matter how hard any of them tried, it was difficult to hold any anger toward their angelic-looking companion. Her blonde hair, blue eyes, and ready smile made being anything but happy around her impossible.

Luther was the last to join their group. Dark-haired and with a personality to match, he was their problem child, even though he swore their simple life was all he wanted in the world. He'd become the camp sheriff. When an injustice occurred, he dealt with it, though with less tact than Damian would prefer sometimes.

Bhren brought the oatmeal over and dished up bowls while they all sat. As a group, they thanked Earth for this bounty and dug in.

Damian passed the letter around as they ate, hoping it wouldn't sour their food like it did his.

"This is ridiculous," Luther said. He waved the letter in the air. "They can't do this."

Wyeth tugged the piece of paper from his hand, taking only seconds to scan it before handing it to his wife. "No one should be able to buy this land. This is part of the Black Hills National Forest. It's protected."

"We thought it was," Valena said.

"Are you sure this information is reliable?"" Gwen, quiet and analytical like her husband, tucked the crazy curls of her red-tinted blonde hair into a cap, then swallowed a spoonful of oatmeal.

Taegar ate with abandon, as if nothing in the world mattered except what she did in this moment. The girl focused on one thing at a time and gave it her all. Damian wondered if she even listened to the conversation.

"I trust the man who sent it. We went to college together and have a lot of the same beliefs about preserving our resources. He chose to further that cause by working as a lawyer in Washington while I took a simpler path. I have to believe this information is accurate."

Luther pounded the table, getting even Taegar's attention. "This is insane. It shouldn't' even be happening."

"Whether or not this can happen is no longer the point," Damian said. "Apparently, it's a done deal. The issue now is what to do about it."

"Who is this Gordon Darcy?" Wyeth asked.

"I did some research this morning. Seems like a corporate type, in it for the money."

"You don't think we'll be able to persuade him of the importance of this place?"

They all grew quiet. Everyone knew what was at

stake here. Damian and Valena had come to this area several years ago and immediately felt the difference. Life was fresher here, more abundant. The trees sang, the breezes whistled, food and vegetation grew better than any other place they'd seen. There was almost a sentience here, a oneness with Earth.

"I think we have to try," Valena said.

Wyeth nodded. "It's the best way to convince someone to change their mind."

Damian sighed. "I guess that means I'm going to Los Angeles."

Valena entwined her arm with his and leaned against him.

Her hair tickled his arms, its sunshine and citrus scent calming him. Almost. With her head on his shoulder, nothing else should matter. Normally, nothing else would, except now the life they'd left behind had been tossed into their laps with a resounding thunk.

"I'll go with you," Valena said quietly.

That suggestion cost his wife a lot. There was no time to drive. They'd have to fly. He and Valena had met when he'd been the guide leading a rescue team deep into the Congo to recover what they'd expected to be bodies from a small plane crash. It had shocked them all that, in the two weeks it took them to get to the wreck, two of the ten people had survived. The pilot, and Valena. They'd had to medicate her to get her back to the states, and she'd never set foot on a plane since.

All those nights torn apart by nightmares. Smitten from the first moment, Damian couldn't have left her if he'd wanted to. So he'd stayed, and he'd held her. Eventually, the nightmares diminished until they were only a rare occurrence during times of high stress.

"You love me so much, you'd get on a plane," he said.

Valena turned to look at him, touching his face. "I love you more."

Damian held her hand to his cheek, soaking up all the tender reverence in her eyes until she snuggled deeper in his embrace, thereby gifting him the time to think. Something she always knew he needed. Valena had saved him even more than he'd saved her. He'd tried so hard for so long to change things. Fighting aqua-cultures that would further taint the oceans, standing strong on the tracks to stop coal trains, even a sit-down to keep a proposed pipeline from crossing through sacred ground. Each time, shot down. Each time, he got angrier. He'd been arrested so many times, he could say without blinking an eye that he had an extensive rap sheet.

Everything he'd tried, whether drastic or diplomatic, had failed. He'd been in a tough place, mentally exhausted and completely demoralized. Moving to South America for those months had proved to be the best thing for him. He'd met Valena, his voice of reason. The one who reminded him that everything mattered, that small changes added up to bigger things.

This, though, the pillaging of sacred land, would be the biggest fight of his life. Damian was certain of it.

"I always want you beside me, my love," he whispered into her hair. "But I think it's better if I make this trip alone."

When her shoulders relaxed, Damian knew his decision had been right. He couldn't put her through that. Not unless there was no other choice.

"I'll go," he said with more vehemence to the group who sat quietly waiting. "Let's see if I can get a meeting with this Gordon Darcy. I'll fly down to Los Angeles and try to convince him how important this land is."

"And I'll load you up with some facts to showcase the importance of leaving this land untainted," Bhren said as he grabbed the laptop.

Damian smiled when everyone nodded their approval. While Damian tended to lead their druid circle, the bigger decisions were generally discussed and decided by the entire group.

"It should be you," Wyeth said. "As long as you can hold on to that rabid temper of yours."

A chuckle rumbled around the table, verifying the hard-won patience Damian had worked to attain.

"That's settled, then." Damian stood. "I'll call Darcy's office and then make arrangements."

His wife stood with him. "I'll clear the dishes for Taegar and check the gardens," she said, giving him a lingering kiss before walking off.

"I've got to check that generator. It's been acting up," Luther said, heading off with a disgruntled wave.

"Financials and world news for me," Wyeth said, pulling out his own laptop and opening it up on the table.

Damian loved the cohesive camaraderie of their circle. Everyone knew what must be done. Everyone had their strengths.

He glanced at Taegar, who prepared to wash dishes.

And their weaknesses.

To keep up with Laurie Ryan news, please join her newsletter. More information can be found at **www.laurieryanauthor.com**.

* 9 7 8 0 9 9 9 5 9 7 7 6 7 *